"You're not only a conspirator! You're a willing participant!"

"Did you *have* to be so—" she paused as words momentarily failed her "—proprietorial?" Lexi's fingers clenched until the knuckles showed white. "You sat there so damned *calmly*, looking at me as if..." She trailed to a frustrated halt, loath to say what Georg had no compunction of voicing.

"...As if I couldn't wait to get you home and into bed?" he completed in a drawling tone, adding with cynical mockery, "Is it so surprising that I might want to?"

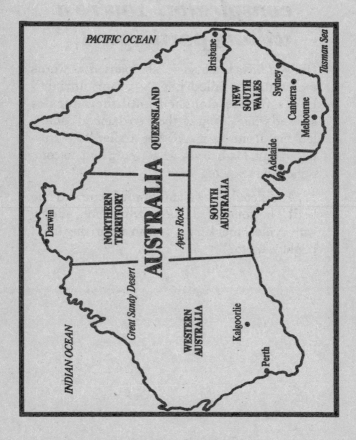

PACIFIC OCEAN

Brisbane

QUEENSLAND

NEW SOUTH WALES

Sydney

Canberra

Melbourne

Tasman Sea

AUSTRALIA

Adelaide

NORTHERN TERRITORY

Ayers Rock

SOUTH AUSTRALIA

Darwin

Great Sandy Desert

WESTERN AUSTRALIA

Kalgoorlie

Perth

INDIAN OCEAN

HELEN BIANCHIN

No Gentle Seduction

Harlequin Books

TORONTO • NEW YORK • LONDON
AMSTERDAM • PARIS • SYDNEY • HAMBURG
STOCKHOLM • ATHENS • TOKYO • MILAN
MADRID • WARSAW • BUDAPEST • AUCKLAND

Harlequin Presents first edition February 1993
ISBN 0-373-11527-X

Original hardcover edition published in 1991
by Mills & Boon Limited

NO GENTLE SEDUCTION

CHAPTER ONE

Hot, humid southern hemispheric temperatures prevailed, shrouding Sydney's tall city buildings in a stultifying summer heat-haze capable of frazzling the most even temperament.

Traffic in all city-bound lanes had slowed to a standstill, and Lexi spared a quick glance at her watch as she waited for the queue of cars to begin moving again.

A faint frown furrowed her smooth brow, and her lacquered nails played out an abstracted tattoo against the steering-wheel as she pondered her brother's telephone call of the previous evening. The serious tone of David's voice had proved vaguely perturbing, and no amount of cajoling had persuaded him to reveal any information.

Lexi shifted gears as the lights changed and she sent the sports car forward with a muted growl from its superb engine.

The movement of air teased tendrils of dark auburn hair loose from its careless knot atop her head, and she lifted a hand to brush them back from her cheek. Designer sunglasses shaded golden hazel eyes, and her attractive fine-boned features drew several admiring glances as she made her way into the city.

A wry smile twisted the edges of her generous mouth in the knowledge that as much of the envious speculation was for the aerodynamic lines of her brother's near-new red Ferrari 348 as it was for the girl driving it. Wealth wasn't everything, she silently derided, and natural good looks could prove a handicap—something she'd discovered to her cost.

Such thoughts were detrimental, and she determinedly shut out the past by deliberately concentrating on negotiating the heavy inner-city traffic.

Ten minutes later a soft sigh of relief escaped her lips as she turned into the car park beneath a towering modern block housing her brother's suite of offices. Using extreme care, she eased the red sports car down two levels and brought it to a smooth halt in its reserved parking bay.

Gathering up her bag, she slid to her feet just as another car pulled into a nearby space, and her eyes widened fractionally at the sight of an almost identical Ferrari. The coincidence of two expensive Italian sports cars parking within such close proximity was highly improbable, and she watched with detached interest as the driver emerged from behind the wheel.

He was tall, she noticed idly, with an enviable breadth of shoulder evident beneath the flawless cut of his jacket, and he moved with the lithe ease of inherent strength. His hair was dark and well-groomed, and the broad-chiselled bone-structure moulded his features into rugged attractiveness.

Features that were vaguely familiar, and yet even as she searched her memory there was no spark of recognition, no name she could retrieve that would identify him.

As if sensing her scrutiny he lifted his head, and she was unprepared for the dark probing gaze that raked her slim curves in analytical appraisal before returning to settle overlong on the soft fullness of her mouth. Then his eyes travelled slowly up to focus on her startled expression.

She felt a surge of rage begin deep inside, and its threatened eruption brought a fiery sparkle to her beautiful eyes. How *dared* he subject her to such blatantly sexual assessment?

Impossibly angry, she turned towards the car, locked the door and activated the alarm, then she crossed to the lifts to jab the call-button with unnecessary force, silently willing any one of three lifts to descend and transport her to the fifteenth floor.

It irked her unbearably that she should still be waiting when he joined her, and she stood silently aloof until a faint hydraulic hiss heralded the arrival of a lift. As soon as as the doors slid open she stepped forward with easy grace into the electronic cubicle, pressed the appropriate digit on the illuminated panel, then stood back in silence, mentally distancing herself from the man's physical presence.

A faint prickle of apprehension feathered the surface of her skin, which was crazy, for he posed no threat. Yet she was frighteningly aware of his studied evaluation, and she hated the elusive alchemy that pulled at her senses. She was damned if she'd give him the satisfaction of returning his gaze. Who did he think he was, for heaven's sake?

A sobering inner voice silently derided that he knew precisely who he was, and without doubt his action was a deliberate attempt to ruffle her composure.

Somehow she expected him to voice any one of several differing phrases men inevitably used as an opening gambit with an attractive woman, and when he didn't the rage within only intensified, for it gave her no opportunity to deliver a scathing response.

It took only seconds to reach the fifteenth floor, but it felt like minutes, and so intense was her need to escape that she stepped from the lift the instant the doors slid open, unable to prevent the feeling that she was fleeing from a predatory animal.

A sensation that was as totally insane as it was out of perspective, she mentally chided as she entered the foyer of her brother's suite of legal offices.

'Good morning, Miss Harrison,' the receptionist greeted warmly. 'Mr Harrison said to go straight through.'

'Thanks,' Lexi proffered with a faint smile as she continued past the central desk and turned down a corridor leading to a large corner office which offered panoramic views of the city and inner harbour.

'David,' she greeted as the door closed behind her, accepting the affectionate brush of her brother's lips against her cheek before she subsided into a nearby chair. 'Thanks for organising my car into the repair shop. I've parked the red monster in its usual space.'

David's eyebrows rose in a gesture of feigned offence. '*Monster*, Lexi?'

A faint grin curved her generous mouth. 'Sorry,' she corrected, aware that the Ferrari represented an unaccustomed flamboyance in his otherwise staid existence as one of Sydney's leading barristers. 'Your magnificent motoring machine.'

As the son and daughter of one of Australia's most respected financial entrepreneurs, they had each achieved success in their own right, choosing to decline any assistance afforded them by virtue of their father's considerable wealth and position.

'Have you any plans for tonight?'

Her eyes widened slightly. 'I can't imagine you need to resort to your sister's company through lack of a suitable female partner.'

His glance was level and strangely watchful as he offered a light bantering response. 'Now that your decree absolute has been granted I thought we might celebrate by having dinner together.'

An entire gamut of emotions flitted in and out of her expressive eyes, and for a moment he glimpsed her pain before a wry, faintly cynical smile tugged the edges of her mouth.

Despite her reluctance, memories sharpened into startling focus. The dissolution of her marriage meant that she no longer bore any affiliation, legal or otherwise, to a man who had deliberately pursued her for the fame of her family name and the considerable fortune he imagined would be his to access at will as the husband of Jonathan Harrison's daughter.

Paul Ellis had epitomised every vulnerable young girl's dream and every caring parent's nightmare, Lexi reflected with grim hindsight. Within weeks of returning to Australia from a two-year working stint in Europe she met Paul at a party, and became instantly attracted to him. Blindly infatuated, she had discounted her father's caution, disregarded

David's advice, and married Paul three months later in a whirl of speculative publicity.

To Jonathan's credit he had concealed his concern and provided a wedding that had proved to be the social event of the year.

Mere days into a Caribbean honeymoon Lexi's dream of marital bliss had begun to fragment as Paul voiced a series of protests. The home her father had presented them with as a wedding gift was considered by Paul as too small for the sort of entertaining he had had in mind, and his disappointment in Jonathan's failure to appoint his son-in-law to the board of directors had been compounded when Lexi had refused to exert any influence in Paul's favour. His sudden enthusiasm for a child had raised doubts in Lexi's mind, and when she had elected to defer pregnancy for a year he'd lost his temper and the rift between them had become irreparable.

Paul, when faced with the *fait accompli* of legal separation, had filed claim for a huge financial settlement and threatened court proceedings if his demands were not met.

One of David's colleagues had conducted such superb legal representation that Paul's case was thrown out of court.

Concentrating on her modelling career, Lexi had declined her father's offer to occupy his prestigious Vaucluse mansion, opting instead to live alone in a beautifully furnished apartment at Darling Point overlooking the inner harbour.

At twenty-five she was considered to be one of Sydney's top models, and work provided a panacea that helped relegate Paul to the past.

The experience had left her with a cynical attitude towards men to such an extent that she chose not to date at all, preferring the company of Jonathan and David on the few occasions it became necessary for her to provide an escort.

Now Lexi met David's steady gaze with equanimity. 'That's the momentous news you wanted to discuss with me in person?'

He was silent for a few long seconds as he chose his words with care. 'Part of it.'

Her eyes widened fractionally at his hesitation.

'Paul has somehow discovered Jonathan is at present undertaking extremely delicate negotiations with a Japanese consortium to finance a proposed tourist resort on Queensland's Gold Coast,' he revealed slowly, and Lexi cast him a puzzled glance.

'In what context can Paul pose any threat?'

'He has made a demand for money.'

'Why?' she demanded at once.

David seemed to take an inordinate amount of time in answering. 'He is threatening to sell his story of the marriage break-up to the Press, detailing how he was discarded by the Harrison family without a cent.' His lips twisted. 'The fact that Paul deliberately set Jonathan's fortune in his sights and preyed upon your emotions is immaterial,' he informed cynically. 'The Press, at Paul's direction, will have a field-day. Especially when it can run a concurrent story of the extent of Jonathan's financial involvement in the Japanese deal.'

Lexi didn't need to be told just how Paul's supposed plight would be highlighted. Without doubt he would portray the injured party to the

hilt, invoking reader sympathy against the pluto-
cratic Harrison family. As long as there was some
basis of fact the truth was unimportant with some
tabloids, and the major criterion was saleable copy.

'But surely the Japanese consortium is astute
enough not to allow personalities to enter into any
business dealings?'

'Indeed,' he agreed drily. 'However, they will
acquire their tourist resort regardless of whether
Jonathan's company is the majority shareholder or
not. There are other viable companies which would
clutch at any straw in their struggle for power.'

Lexi didn't need to be enlightened as to her ex-
husband's duplicity. 'The price for his silence is a
financial settlement,' Lexi concluded, her eyes
hardening until they resembled dark topaz. 'A
settlement he was legally unable to obtain when we
separated.'

'Unfortunately it isn't that simple,' David
declared slowly. 'Jonathan is as yet unaware of
Paul's intention. With your help I intend to keep
it that way.'

Her eyes flashed with brilliant gold. 'Paul has no
scruples whatsoever, and I'm damned if I'll allow
you or Jonathan to pay Paul what amounts to
blackmail on my account. It would only be the
beginning, and you know it!'

David moved to stand beside the wide expanse
of plate-glass, his expression pensive and incredibly
solemn as he appeared to admire the view. After
what seemed an age he turned towards her and
thrust hands into his trouser pockets.

'The Japanese deal is important to Jonathan.' He
effected a negligible shrug. 'But its failure or success

is immaterial in the long term. There are other deals, other opportunities. However, in this particular issue the element of timing is crucial, and with Jonathan's health at stake I'll do anything in my power to prevent him from suffering any unnecessary stress.'

A painful hand clutched at her heart, and her voice became husky with concern. 'What's wrong with Jonathan?' Her eyes clung to his. 'Why haven't you told me?'

'Because there was no point until all the tests were conclusive,' David said gently. 'His only option is a triple bypass, and surgery is scheduled for the beginning of January. Timed,' he added wryly, 'at Jonathan's insistence, to coincide with the anticipated conclusion of the Japanese negotiations. In the meantime it's essential he leads a quiet life with minimum stress.' He drew a deep breath as he surveyed her pale, stricken features. 'I hardly need to tell you what effect Paul's threatened publicity will have on Jonathan if we're unable to prevent it from erupting prior to surgery.'

The fact that her indomitable human dynamo of a father was victim of a heart disease was more than she could bear. 'It's that serious?'

David reached out and caught hold of her hand. 'You must know he'll have the best surgeon,' he reassured gently. 'And such operations are now considered routine.'

Lexi could only look at him blankly, her mind filling with conflicting images and an unassailable anger that anything Paul attempted might damage her father's health. 'What possible solution have you come up with?' she managed at last.

David seemed to take his time, then offered quietly, 'Paul's adverse publicity attempt will look extremely foolish if you were already heavily involved, even engaged, to a man who is sufficiently wealthy to finance the necessary fifty-one-per-cent stake. A man who could present the role of adoring fiancé with conviction.' Seeing her silent scepticism, he lifted his hand in a dismissive gesture as he sought to assure. 'With careful orchestration and the right publicity we could ensure that any demands Paul sought were seen to be merely a case of sour grapes.'

'Since I'm not romantically involved with anyone, just *who* do you propose to link me with?' she queried with deceptive calm, then said with categoric certainty, 'It won't work.'

'It has to work,' David insisted. 'I can provide sufficient delaying tactics for a week or two on the premise of considering Paul's demands.'

'And the man, David? Just who is this paragon who will give his time to act out a charade?' A faint bitterness crept into her voice. 'And what's *his* price?'

'Georg Nicolaos,' he revealed slowly. 'And there is no price.'

'I find that difficult to believe,' she replied with scepticism. 'Everything has a price.'

'Jonathan's association with the Nicolaos family is well known. He has entered into several joint financial ventures with Alex and Georg Nicolaos in the past. It will come as no surprise if, now that your divorce from Paul is final, Georg Nicolaos is seen escorting you to a variety of functions during the run-down to the festive season.' A faint smile tugged the corners of his mouth. 'It will be alleged in the gossip columns that you and Georg have enjoyed a clandestine relationship for some time, and now that you're legally free Georg is losing no time in staking his claim.'

'Are Alex and Georg Nicolaos involved in this particular venture?'

'Yes.'

'And what if Paul suspects it's merely a smokescreen?'

'I will utilise all my legal ability to persuade him we're more likely to take a magnanimous view of his demands now you're considering marriage with Georg. I can gain time with negotiations by insisting that Paul sign a document indicating he has no further financial claim on acceptance of an agreed amount.'

She gave him a look of scandalised disbelief. 'So you *do* intend to pay him?'

'A token sum, commensurate with the length of time he was married to you.' His good-looking features hardened into a mask of distaste. 'Added to the car and furniture he spirited out of the house within hours of your leaving him, the total value will be more than generous under the circumstances.' His expression gentled. 'Four weeks, Lexi—five at the most. Surely it's not too much to ask?'

She hesitated, unwilling to voice her own reluctance for fear it would sound ungrateful in light of the caring support her father and brother had each given her during the past two years. 'I can hardly refuse, can I?' she said at last, and glimpsed the relieved satisfaction in his eyes.

'In that case, I'll contact Georg and arrange for him to meet us this evening.'

So soon? Yet logic demanded there was no reason for delay.

Almost as if he sensed her reserve, he gave her hand a reassuring squeeze. 'I'll call for you at six-thirty.'

She possessed a wardrobe filled with designer clothes, and she mentally reviewed them in an attempt to make an appropriate selection. 'I imagine you require me to present a dazzling image?'

'You look fantastic in anything.'

'Now that's what I call brotherly love,' Lexi accepted with a contrived smile. Sparing her watch a quick glance, she rose to her feet and delved into her bag to extract a set of keys which she pressed into his hand. 'Thanks for the loan of the Ferrari.'

David tossed them down on to his desk and reached into a nearby drawer. 'Here's yours. It's parked on level three, close to the lifts.'

'Give me the bill,' she insisted, 'and I'll write you a cheque.'

He made no demur and merely extracted the itemised account, watching as she wrote in the amount and attached her signature with unaffected flair.

Collecting her keys, she made her way towards the door. 'I have a modelling assignment at eleven. Jacques will have a fit if I'm late.'

The Mercedes sports car purred to life at the first turn of the key, and Lexi exited the car park, then headed towards the eastern suburbs.

The address she'd been given was for a restaurant venue in Double Bay whose patron had generously donated to charity the cost of providing food for the seventy ticket-paying guests.

It was, Jacques assured, a long-standing annual event for which the particular charity involved was dependently grateful.

Parking was achieved with ease, and Lexi locked up, activating the car alarm before walking towards the main street.

She located the discreet restaurant display-board without difficulty, and traversed a wide curving staircase to the main entrance, where an elegantly gowned hostess greeted and directed her to a make-shift changing-room.

'Lexi, you're late,' a harassed voice announced the instant she entered the small room, and she checked her watch with a faintly raised eyebrow.

'By less than a minute,' she protested as she deftly began discarding her outer clothes. 'The fashion parade isn't due to begin for another half-hour.'

'Time which must be spent perfecting the hair and make-up, *oui*?'

The models were due to take to the catwalk at precisely eleven-thirty, displaying a variety of exclusive labels for an hour, after which lunch would be served, followed by customary speeches and the giving of a few token awards.

Thank heaven today's modelling assignment was being held indoors in air-conditioned comfort, Lexi consoled herself more than an hour later as she hurriedly discarded an elegantly tailored suit and reached for a superb evening gown, the final selection in a superb fashion range.

Yesterday had involved a beach, searing sun, hot sand, and a gathering of ogling, wolf-whistling young men intent on upsetting her composure.

Modelling was hard work, and often the antithesis of its projected glamorous image, Lexi mused as she took her cue and moved out on to the small makeshift stage. Her hazel-gold eyes were wide and clear, and she portrayed graceful dignity as she took to the catwalk, pausing momentarily as she executed a series of choreographed movements; then she returned to the stage to effect one final turn before slipping through the curtain to backstage.

'The restaurateur has set a table aside for those of you who wish to eat,' Jacques informed them as he carefully slid the last garment into its protective cover. 'Of course, there is no obligation to stay.'

The three other models opted to remain, while Lexi shook her head in silent negation. 'I can't. I have a dental appointment in half an hour.'

He gave a typical Gallic shrug. 'Tomorrow at three, Lexi,' he reminded her, and she nodded in acquiescence as she cast her reflection a quick glance before collecting her bag.

'I must fly, or I'll be late.'

Slipping out of the changing-room, Lexi quickly manoeuvred her way between tables, inadvertently bumping into a solid masculine frame which seemed to appear out of nowhere.

Her hand clutched his arm in an instinctive attempt to steady herself, and a faint smile parted her lips accompanied by a few words in murmured apology.

Words that froze in the back of her throat as she recognised the man with whom she'd shared a lift only a few hours earlier.

This close she could see the fine lines fanning out from the corners of his eyes, the deep groove slashing each cheek.

He possessed an animalistic sense of power, as well as an indefinable sensual quality that was infinitely dangerous to any sensible woman's peace of mind.

There was a degree of mocking amusement evident in the depths of his gaze, and Lexi became aware that she was still clutching his arm.

She snatched her hand away as if burned by fire, and her eyes flared to a brilliant gold as she regained the power of speech. 'I'm sorry. Excuse me,' she added in a huskily spoken afterthought as she made to move past him.

'You are not staying?'

His drawled query held the faintest accent, and the sound of it sent a tiny shiver of alarm scudding down the length of her spine.

'No.'

His gaze was steady, his brown eyes dark, inscrutable depths in which it would be all too easy to become lost, and there could be no doubt that he possessed sufficient sensual expertise to melt the hardest heart.

But not hers, she assured herself silently. Definitely not hers. She'd travelled that particular road before, and there was no way she intended being hurt again. By *any* man.

He made no comment, and merely inclined his head in silent mocking acceptance of her decision.

The desperate need to get away from him surprised her, and she lifted a hand to push back the length of her hair in a gesture that was born from nervous tension.

A fact that was unsettling, given her exclusive schooling, she acknowledged as she made her way towards the foyer. And after her disastrously short marriage to Paul she had managed to acquire a protective façade she considered virtually impregnable.

It was after five when Lexi entered her luxurious Darling Point apartment, and her arms were laden with an assortment of brightly coloured carrier-bags that held Christmas gifts for Jonathan and David, as well as an exquisite new perfume she'd bought for herself.

With a sigh of relief she closed the door behind her, eased off her shoes, then carried her purchases through to the spare bedroom. From there she made her way into the kitchen and poured herself a long cool drink of orange juice, then she drifted into the lounge and sank into one of several soft leather chairs.

It had been an unsettling day, fraught with surprises, and she needed ten minutes in which to relax and *think*.

Blind dating—if dining with Georg Nicolaos could be termed that—was something in which she'd never indulged, and she was reluctant to begin, even given such an essentially worthy cause.

Any choice she might have in the matter was a mere fallacy, for there *was* no choice, she decided wryly. Somehow she had to endure being in the constant company of a man she'd never met for the next five weeks; to smile and laugh, and generally give the impression that she was relieved and delighted that their romance, which had supposedly been kept under wraps for months, was now out in the open.

Without doubt it would tax her acting ability to the limit.

With a sigh of resignation she stretched her arms above her head and flexed her shoulders, then rose to her feet and made her way into the bedroom, where she stripped, and took a shower in the adjoining *en suite* bathroom.

Lexi was ready a few minutes before six-thirty, her long hair confined into a knot atop her head from which she deliberately teased free a few soft-curling tendrils. Make-up was deliberately understated, with the accent on subtle shadings of eyeshadow, a touch of blusher, and soft clear rose colouring her lips. The gown she'd chosen was black with a cleverly designed ruched bodice and figure-hugging skirt. It came with a stole which she casually draped across her shoulders, and her feet were encased in black Jourdan slender-heeled shoes.

'Beautiful,' David complimented warmly when she opened the door at his summons.

'Thanks,' she accepted without guile as she preceded him into the lounge. 'Would you like a drink?'

'I told Georg we'd meet him at seven.'

Lexi cast him a quick glance before collecting her evening-bag from a nearby mahogany table. 'In that case, I guess we'd better not keep him waiting.'

Double Bay was a popular 'in' place to eat, hosting a variety of exclusive restaurants, and it wasn't until David led her to a familiar flight of stairs that she realised their destination.

'I was here this morning on a modelling assignment.'

'Really? Georg is known to favour a few worthy charity organisations.'

A brief flicker of surprise lit her features. 'Georg Nicolaos owns the restaurant?'

'It belongs to the Nicolaos family,' David corrected. 'Georg assumed a personal interest in it after the death of his father. If you remember, Alex and I attended university together.'

A darkly handsome figure sprang to mind, formidable and intensely Greek. 'I seem to recollect hearing Alex had married.' A faint gleam sparkled in the depths of her eyes. 'His wife has my sympathy.'

'Dear lord, *why*?'

Lexi gave a husky laugh. 'Oh, for heaven's sake, David! Alex is one of the most frighteningly sexy men I've met. The woman who managed to snare him must be quite something.'

'Samantha is charming,' David allowed, before giving his name to the hostess at the desk.

'Ah, yes, Mr Harrison.' Her smile was practised, bright, and deferential. 'Mr Nicolaos has instructed me to let him know the moment you arrive. If you'd care to follow me, I'll direct you to your table. Mr Nicolaos will join you shortly.'

'You seem to be very much in favour,' Lexi teased minutes after they had taken their seats, and David effected a self-deprecatory shrug.

'I've known the family a long time. Alex waited tables between college and university semesters in the days when his father headed the restaurant. As did Georg and Anna.'

'I find it strange that, although I've met Alex on a number of occasions over the years, I have yet to meet his brother.'

David leaned well back in his chair, a habit he unconsciously adopted whenever he was about to choose his words with care. Lexi wondered if he was aware of it, and why he should do so now.

'Perhaps because Alex chooses to adopt a stand on certain political issues, and enjoys a prominent social existence.'

'And Georg doesn't?' she queried idly.

'Not to the same degree.'

Her eyelids flicked wide. 'Why? Is he a recluse? Or does he not enjoy the company of women?'

David's gleaming humour was somehow directed to a point somewhere beyond her left shoulder.

'On the contrary,' a deep slightly accented, vaguely familiar voice interjected in a silky drawl. 'I very much enjoy the opposite sex.'

Lexi turned slowly to find her worst fears were confirmed, and a silent scream of rejection rose against the irony of fate that Georg Nicolaos and the driver of the red Ferrari were one and same.

CHAPTER TWO

LEXI'S eyes flared briefly in silent resentment as David effected an introduction.

'Mr Nicolaos,' Lexi acknowledged, hating the way her stomach began to knot in sheer reaction to his presence.

'*Georg*, please,' he insisted, holding her gaze a few seconds longer than was necessary before switching his attention to the man seated opposite. 'David.'

A waiter appeared the instant Georg folded his lengthy frame into a chair, and he hovered with intent solicitude as his employer enquired about his guests' choice of wine while Lexi sat stiffly upright as every last nerve-ending tingled alive in silent antipathy.

Not even in her wildest imagination had she envisaged being placed in the invidious position of having to act out a charade with someone of Georg Nicolaos's calibre.

Part of her demanded an escape *now*, while she still had the courage to do so. Except that she was impossibly bound to remain, and she viewed him surreptitiously under the guise of perusing the menu.

In his late thirties, he managed without effort to portray a dramatic mesh of blatant masculinity and elemental ruthlessness—a facet that was obviously a family trait, she decided uncharitably, recalling Alex's formidable features.

The menu was extensive, and she opted for a chicken consommé, followed it with a salad, and waived dessert in favour of the cheeseboard.

'I can't persuade you to sample even one dish from our selection of Greek cuisine?'

Lexi met Georg's dark gaze, and was unable to read anything from his expression. His faint smile held a degree of warmth and was doubtless aimed to put her at ease. Yet beneath the façade she detected a lurking cynicism, and it rankled.

Her eyes held his with deliberately cool regard. 'Thank you, but no,' she refused quietly.

'Another occasion, perhaps?'

She wanted to tell him that there would be no other occasion, but the reality of the next few weeks emerged with vivid clarity.

Lifting her glass to her lips, she savoured its excellent contents, then set it down on to the table, unconsciously tracing the patterned cloth with the tip of her elegantly shaped nail.

Mockery appeared to be her only defence, and she utilised it mercilessly. 'Do we each bring out our figurative engagement books, and consult?'

A gleam of humour sharpened his dark eyes. 'You have your engagement book with you?'

It was crazy to feel so vulnerable, yet she was supremely conscious of every single breath, and it wasn't a sensation she enjoyed.

'Like the advertisement for a well-known credit card,' she responded, 'I never leave home without it.'

'For tomorrow night,' Georg drawled, 'I have tickets for the opera.'

Lexi shook her head. 'I have a photographic modelling session tomorrow afternoon.'

'Which is due to finish—when?'

She effected a faint shrug. 'Five, six,' she hazarded. 'Maybe later. Peter is a perfectionist. He'll take as many shots as he needs to capture precisely the right image.'

'Dinner is obviously out. I'll collect you at seven-thirty.'

She regarded him coolly. 'I could have made other plans.' She heard David's audible intake of breath and registered his protest before he had the opportunity to voice the words.

'Lexi——'

'Perhaps you could check?' Georg interceded in a deep, faintly accented drawl, and an icy chill feathered across the surface of her skin.

Lexi knew she was behaving badly, yet she was unable to prevent herself from searching for her pocket diary and riffling through its pages until she reached the appropriate one. 'Drinks with Elaine, seven o'clock,' she read out, then spared him an apparently regretful glance. 'Sorry. Not the opera.' A shaft of remorse prompted her to offer a slight smile. 'Unless I miss the first act and join you during the second?'

'Alternatively, we could both miss the first act,' Georg declared silkily.

It was a clash of wills, and she was determined to win. 'I wouldn't dream of allowing you to make such a concession. If you let me have the ticket I'll meet you there.'

'Surely you could cancel Elaine?' David intervened, shooting her a cautionary look that ordinarily she would have heeded.

'Arrangements were made weeks ago for a number of friends to meet for a few pre-Christmas drinks,' she explained. 'If I opt out she'll be hurt. Besides,' she qualified, unable to prevent a faint tinge of bitterness entering her voice, 'once my supposed romance with Georg hits the gossip columns there will be no peace at all. At least permit me another day of relative freedom.'

'I should remind you that Georg is under no obligation whatsoever,' David declared heavily.

'Perhaps not,' she tempered sweetly. 'Although, business-wise, I doubt if either Alex or Georg wants this particular deal to fall through. Therefore, Georg *does* have an interest. Am I not right?' She spared her brother a winsome smile before switching her attention to his companion. 'Unless, of course, he's bored with life and not averse to a little subterfuge by way of adventure. Is that the reason you've agreed to act as a mythical knight in shining armour, Georg?' She deliberately gave his name its correct phonetic pronunciation, so that it fell from her lips as 'Jorj'.

His eyes swept her features in raking assessment, then locked with hers for a brief instant before assuming an expression of bland inscrutability. 'My life is far from boring,' he acknowledged with velvet-smoothness, although only a fool would have failed to perceive the steel evident.

'Yet you are willing to reorganise your social life to the extent of putting it entirely on hold for a month.' She let her eyes travel at will over each and every one of his visible features in an appraisal that was meant to diffuse the sheer overwhelming presence of the man. 'Your current—er—companion,' she accorded with delicate emphasis, 'must be extremely understanding.'

Georg regarded her steadily until she almost felt impelled to wrench her gaze away from those fathomless dark eyes, then his eyelids lowered slightly, successfully masking his expression as he proffered a faintly mocking smile.

'You're a very attractive young woman,' he drawled. 'Being your escort for a few weeks in an attempt to perpetrate an illusion will provide no hardship at all.'

It was as well the waiter arrived at that precise moment with their starter, and Lexi spooned the excellent chicken consommé with little appetite, and merely picked at her salad.

The wine helped soothe her nerves, although she refused to allow her glass to be refilled and opted for chilled water throughout the remainder of the meal.

It was almost ten when David indicated that they should leave, and Lexi experienced considerable relief that the evening was almost over.

'Your ticket for the opera,' Georg indicated as he withdrew a slim envelope from his jacket pocket and handed it to her.

She took care that their fingers didn't touch, aware from the faint gleam of amusement evident that he *knew*. 'I'm not sure what time I'll get there,' she ventured, determined not to rush away from Elaine's party before she was ready.

'Try to make it before the final act,' he advised in a cynical drawl. 'And take a taxi,' he added. 'We'll go on to a night-club afterwards.'

Her lashes swept up as she cast him a cool glance. 'Is that necessary?'

'It is if we're to be seen together, photographed and captioned in the gossip columns.' His smile was totally without humour. 'Our supposed "romance" won't have much credence if we depart in separate vehicles.'

She felt her stomach give a sickening lurch at the reality of what she was about to undertake. Yet any visible sign of apprehension was unthinkable, and she tilted her chin fractionally as she proffered a brilliant smile. 'I'll endeavour to dazzle.'

'You appear to do that without effort,' Georg accorded drily as he rose to his feet, and Lexi followed suit, collecting her evening-bag as he escorted them both to the lobby.

'Really, Lexi,' David chastised her the instant they were out of earshot. 'You were incredibly rude——'

'I know everything you're going to say,' she intercepted a trifle wearily, glad that they had reached the street. 'Treat it as a temporary aberration.' Her voice assumed an unaccustomed asperity. 'I just hate the degree of my own involvement in this ill-fated scheme.' Especially with someone like Georg Nicolaos, a tiny voice taunted.

David shot her a perceptive look. 'Georg is unlikely to proposition you, if that's your concern.'

Oh, *David*, she longed to deride him. If only you knew how emotionally insecure I feel—how afraid

I am to get close to *any* man, even if it's only to participate in an inglorious charade!

Yet she said nothing, and merely walked at his side to the car, opting to remain pensively silent as he drove her the short distance to her apartment block.

'Ring me at the office on Wednesday. Jonathan mentioned something about our both joining him at home for dinner.' His kindly eyes pierced hers in the dim interior of the car. 'Georg will make a welcome guest. Invite him along.'

She was caught in a trap, and already she could feel the first tinge of pain. 'I'll mention it,' she compromised, slipping easily from the low-slung vehicle the instant it pulled to a halt. 'Goodnight.'

'Darling, *must* you?'

The words appeared to be sincere, but in reality masked boredom and lack of interest, and Lexi wondered why she'd stayed at Elaine's party for so long.

Sheer perversity, born from a desire to tread the edge of Georg Nicolaos's self-control; something that was akin to total madness, she decided as she declared that she really *must* leave.

'I'll just say goodnight to Elaine,' she murmured, then drifted towards a group of three women deep in animated conversation near the door.

Kisses, a few shared hugs, the exchanged avowals to enjoy a really great 'Chrissie', then Lexi managed to slip away.

The taxi she'd ordered was parked outside, waiting, and the driver merely shrugged in complacent resignation as she directed him to the Opera House.

Lexi checked the ticket—something she hadn't bothered to do until now—and saw that the reservation was for *Madame Butterfly*.

The torturous and incredibly sad aspects of love, no matter how beautifully enacted, could hardly be her favoured selection. Yet a quirk of sardonic irony permitted her to see humour in the unwanted parable. The question that sprang immediately to mind was whether Georg Nicolaos's choice was deliberate or merely happenstance.

Some thirty minutes later Lexi was led unobtrusively to a section which comprised some of the best seats in the house, and with a murmured apology she moved along the aisle and sank down into the reserved space.

Her hand was captured almost at once, and she instinctively pulled against the strength of Georg's fingers as he threaded them through her own.

'Seated behind us, to your left, is Anaïs Pembleton,' he cautioned softly as he leaned closer, and she closed her eyes in frustration that one of the city's leading matrons should have chosen tonight of all nights to visit the opera. Worse, that the society doyenne should be seated in the immediate vicinity. Sharp-eyed and acid-tongued, Anaïs Pembleton had a nose for gossip to the extent that she was accorded the status of the uncrowned queen of the gossip-mongers. Lexi hardly needed Georg to remind her to behave.

'How...opportune,' she murmured, hating his close proximity, the faint helplessness at having her hand enclosed within his own, and the sheer animal magnetism he managed to exude without any seeming effort.

'Try to smile,' he drawled, and she could sense his cynical amusement. 'The curtain is about to fall.'

A minute was all she had to prepare herself, and for one brief second her eyes felt incredibly large, their poignant depths strangely dry as she fought to quell the faint trembling of her lips.

'Would you prefer to remain seated?'

He was quite devastating when he deliberately set out to charm and she endeavoured to match the warmth reflected in his smile. 'Could we mingle in the foyer?' At least then she could move around, and there was always the chance she might meet an acquaintance, thus providing an opportunity to focus her attention on someone other than *him*.

Georg rose to his feet without a word, leading her through a throng of fashionably attired men and women.

Lexi had chosen to wear a formal gown of rich red velvet, its body-hugging lines emphasising her soft feminine curves. A wrap in matching velvet added undeniable elegance, and she'd utilised two side-combs to sweep the hair back from her face. Her only jewellery was a diamond pendant on a slim gold chain, and matching ear-studs.

'A drink?' he queried as they reached the foyer.

'Lime and soda, with a dash of bitters.'

'Ice?'

'Please,' she acceded, watching as a waiter appeared at their side as if by magic.

Georg Nicolaos emanated an infinite degree of power of a kind that commanded instant attention.

Yet there was no arrogance apparent, just a compelling omnipotence that scorned all forms of weakness.

It was little wonder that women were held enthralled by him, she perceived wryly. Even if he wasn't extraordinarily wealthy, he would still manage to snare most feminine hearts.

He smiled, and deep grooves slashed his cheeks. 'How was the party?'

She looked at him carefully, analysing the broad-sculptured bone-structure, the steady wide-spaced dark eyes. 'Fine.' A faint moue appeared momentarily, then it was gone, and she effected a slight shrug. 'Am I now supposed to enquire about your day?'

'Are you in the least interested?' he queried, watching as she lifted her glass and took a small sip.

'I know very little about you,' Lexi ventured, and her eyes flared as he reached out and threaded his fingers through her own. Her initial instinct to pull free was thwarted, and she retaliated with a surreptitious dig from her long hard nails.

'Why, Georg,' a breathy feminine voice intruded, 'how wonderful to see you! Are you going on to the club afterwards?'

Lexi turned slowly and met a vision of brunette perfection attired in black silk that shrieked an exclusive designer label only the favoured few could afford.

'Louise,' he acknowledged, then performed an introduction.

'Your face is familiar, yet I'm sure we've never met,' the brunette declared with a faint frown.

'Lexi is a model,' Georg revealed smoothly, clasping Lexi's hand even more firmly within his own.

The gesture didn't go unnoticed, and Lexi caught the sharpness apparent in Louise's beautiful blue eyes before the expression was carefully masked.

'Harrison. Are you any relation to Jonathan Harrison?'

There was no point in denying the truth. 'His daughter.'

There was instant, inevitable knowledge evident in the other girl's exquisite features. 'Of course. Now I remember. Your marriage and divorce achieved notoriety in the Press.'

During the past two years Lexi had encountered several occasions such as this one, and had become accustomed to dealing with them. Pride lifted her chin, and her lashes swept down to form a partial protective veil. 'At the time it was a seven-day wonder,' she allowed with quiet dignity.

'A sensation,' Louise corrected with sweet emphasis. 'No sooner was the honeymoon over than so was the marriage.' There was a delicate pause as she waited for Lexi's comment, and when none was forthcoming a glitter of malice appeared briefly before it was quickly masked. 'I imagine it was a difficult time for you.'

Lexi felt she owed no one an explanation, and any comment was superfluous.

'Finish your drink, darling,' Georg drawled, 'and we'll return to our seats.'

Lexi heard the cool bland words, yet they barely registered. *'Darling'?*

'You'll excuse us, Louise?'

Lexi's glass was taken from her hand, and beneath her startled gaze she watched as he calmly placed it, only half-empty, down on to a nearby tray.

Within seconds she found herself being drawn towards the auditorium.

'Do you mind unshackling me?' she demanded in a vicious undertone.

'Behave,' Georg adjured quietly. 'If you continue to struggle you'll only hurt yourself.'

'Damn you, let me go! I'm not a child in need of a restraining hand!'

It was a relief to reach their seats, and she was glad of the subdued lighting. It hid the faint angry flush that lay along her cheekbones and the glittering sparkle in the depths of her eyes.

A furtive but strong tug of her hand did no good at all, and the breath stilled in her throat as she felt the slight pressure of his thumb caressing the fast-pulsing veins at her wrist.

She turned towards him, only to find he had leaned sideways and his face was mere inches from her own.

'Have you no shame?' Lexi hissed, incensed almost beyond words as she saw his attention deliberately centre on the fullness of her mouth.

Slowly his eyes travelled up to meet her own, and she had to restrain herself from hitting him at the glimpse of mocking amusement apparent in their depths.

'None whatsoever.'

It was as well that the house lights dimmed then as the curtain rose for the third and final act, she decided vengefully. Otherwise she would have been tempted to slap his hateful face!

The dramatic conclusion to Cio-cio-san's tragic romance with an American naval officer was splendidly performed, and the depth and agonising pathos portrayed brought a lump to Lexi's throat as she was held enraptured by the sheer magical spell of the Japanese girl's emotional trauma.

Lexi was unable to prevent thoughts of her own disenchantment with Paul, the loss of trust, the deliberate deception, and her eyes began to ache as she sought to suppress the tell-tale shimmer of tears.

Dear heaven, what was the matter with her? Why tonight, of all night, did she have to fall prey to such maudlin emotions?

Because, an inner voice taunted, you've been thrust into a damnable situation where you're forced to conform to a set of circumstances with a man whose sense of purpose is nothing less than daunting.

Members of the Press were waiting in the foyer to photograph the more famous of the opera devotees, and any hope Lexi held for being able to slip away undetected died even before it was born as camera lenses were thrust in her face and a hard-voiced journalist asked a host of probing questions.

Georg handled it all with urbane charm, and Lexi had merely to smile. At last they were free, and she moved quickly at Georg's side as he led her through a side-door and down into the car park.

It wasn't until they were in the car that she began to relax, although her relief was short-lived as she realised that the Ferrari was heading towards the city.

'I'd prefer to go home, if you don't mind.'

He turned his head slightly and spared her a brief, inflexible glance, then concentrated on negotiating the traffic. 'Half an hour at the club will provide the opportunity for more publicity.' His voice assumed a silky drawl. 'I think you'll agree that's the main objective?'

'I would have thought the news hounds would be satisfied with our appearance at the opera,' she offered with a touch of cynicism, becoming impossibly angry when he offered no comment.

She maintained an icy silence until Georg brought the car to a halt in a city car park, and she slid out from the passenger seat, then closed the door with a firm clunk before flicking him a cool aloof glance.

'Thirty minutes,' she vouchsafed. 'Any longer and I'll call a taxi.'

He could annihilate her in a second. It was there in his eyes, the firm set of his mouth, and Lexi wondered at her own temerity in acting like a spoilt bitch.

'We either do this properly, or we won't do it at all,' Georg stated with chilling cynicism.

The desire to rage against his implacability was paramount, and her eyes warred openly with his, longing to consign him to hell. Never could she remember feeling so intensely angry; not even with Paul.

Without a word she moved away from the car and began walking towards the flight of stairs leading up to the carpeted lobby.

It wasn't surrender—more a case of restrained capitulation, she assured herself, supremely conscious of several patrons waiting for a lift to transport them to the trendy night-club situated on the top floor of the building.

The venue was crowded, attesting to its popularity, and intent on playing host to a plethora of 'beautiful' people who were more interested in being 'seen' as they flitted from table to table in the pursuit of compliments regarding their designer-label clothes and the success of their latest business dealings.

'What would you like to drink?'

Lexi's eyes flashed with a mixture of resentment and silent antipathy for one brief second before long thick lashes swept down to form a protective veil. 'Do I look as if I need one?'

'You look,' Georg drawled in a silky undertone, 'as if you've been thrown into a den of lions.'

He was too perceptive by far! The music was loud, the band excellent, and she let her gaze rove round the room, recognising at least half a dozen familiar faces.

'Georg, you decided to come. Louise said you would, but I hardly dared believed her.'

Lexi turned slightly to encounter an exquisite blonde whose appearance was as sexually blatant as her voice.

'Brigitte,' he acknowledged in an amused drawl. With casual ease he curved a possessive arm around Lexi's waist as he effected an introduction, and it took considerable effort on her part to proffer a brilliant smile.

'Are there any women you *don't* know?' she queried the instant Brigitte moved out of earshot.

'Shall we attempt the dance-floor?'

Oh, he was the very limit! 'Do I have any choice?'

Without a word he drew her towards the centre of the room, and she instinctively stiffened as he caught her close.

His hold was hardly conventional, and she wanted to tear herself away. *Pretend,* an inner voice chided. In all probability he no more wants to dance with you than you do with him! So just close your eyes, and follow his lead.

Except that it wasn't that simple. The cool crisp smell of his cologne mingled with the slight muskiness emanating from his skin, stirring alive an elusive chemistry that made her want to move even closer within his grasp.

It was almost as if she were in the grip of some magnetic force, and she gave an imperceptible start as she felt the brush of his lips against her temple.

Her eyes flew wide open, and for one brief second those brilliant depths mirrored a mixture of pain and outrage before assuming an opaqueness that shuttered the windows to her soul.

It was totally insane, but she felt as if somehow with subtle manipulation Georg Nicolaos had assumed control of her life, and it rankled unbearably.

Sheer will-power helped her survive the next half-hour as they alternately drifted round the dance-floor and paused to converse with fellow guests.

Lexi even managed to smile as they bade good-night to a few of Georg's acquaintances, and she suffered his arm at her waist as they traversed the lobby, rode the lift and ultimately reached the car.

Safely seated inside, she simply maintained an icy silence as he fired the engine and sent the car purring towards street level.

Traffic was moderately light, and she stared sightlessly out of the windscreen as he headed for Darling Point.

Lexi reached for the door-handle the instant the Ferrari slid to a halt outside the entrance to her apartment block, and she cast Georg a look of disbelief as he switched off the ignition and calmly stepped out of the car.

'Where do you think you're going?'

'Escorting you safely indoors, where you'll make me some coffee, which will take at least half an hour to consume.'

'The hell I will!' She was so furious she could have hit him, and she wrenched her arm in a fruitless attempt to be free of him. 'I'm tired, and I want to go to bed. I have an early-morning photographic shoot, and I need to look good!'

He was leading her inexorably towards the entrance. What was more, he'd calmly retrieved her security-coded card and a set of keys from her hand. Before she could voice any further protest they were indoors and heading towards the lift-shaft.

'A car tailed us all the way here,' Georg informed her silkily. 'Without doubt an enthusiastic journalist from one of the less salubrious tabloids.' He jabbed the call-button and the doors immediately slid open. 'We've brought a supposedly clandestine affair out into the open, and it will seem contradictory if I merely drop you off and drive away, don't you think?'

Safely inside the cubicle, she let loose some of her rage. 'I could have a headache!'

His hard, rough-chiselled features assumed mocking cynicism. 'Have you?'

'You, David—this whole wretched farce gives me a headache!' Lexi retorted waspishly.

The lift came to a halt, and she stepped quickly out and headed towards the furthest of two doors situated to the left.

Georg was there before her, the key in the lock, and she turned to face him as soon as the door closed shut.

All the pent-up fury erupted with potent force, and, unbidden, her hand snaked towards his face, the small explosion of sound seeming to rebound in the silence of the room.

His eyes gleamed with glittery anger, and for one horrifying second she thought he meant to strike her back.

He stood curiously still, in perfect control, yet Lexi only barely managed to suppress an involuntary shiver. Never in her life had she felt so threatened, and she unconsciously held her breath, her eyes wide and unblinking as she stood transfixed in mesmeric horror.

'Does that make you feel better?' Georg drawled with dangerous softness. He conducted a slow, deliberate appraisal of each and every one of her physical attributes, and she almost died at the expression in those dark eyes as they returned to meet her own, reflecting a savage ruthlessness that made her want to turn and run.

'Be warned,' he cautioned with icy remoteness. 'I will not be your whipping boy.' His eyes speared hers, activating an angry defiance deep within, turning her golden-hazel eyes a brilliant topaz with the sheer force of it.

'And I won't tolerate any tyrannical behaviour,' she retaliated, uncaring of the tiny flaring from the centre of those hard brown eyes.

'I am here in the guise of an ally, not your enemy,' he reminded her implacably.

'And it would be much easier if I were amenable?' She felt as if she were on a roller-coaster, experiencing the tumult of emotional fear and exhilaration that went with the thrill of courting danger.

'While I can understand your aversion to men in general,' he drawled, 'you would be advised to remember that I am not cast from the same mould as your ex-husband.'

'That doesn't mean I have to like you.' Her attempt at cool anger failed dismally in the face of his mocking cynicism.

'My dear Lexi, you don't know me well enough to judge.'

She wanted to lash out, physically *hit* him, and be damned to the consequences. One transgression had been ignored, and she knew without doubt that another would bring retaliation of a kind she'd be wise to avoid.

'Will you please leave?'

'I'll make the coffee.'

He appeared so indomitable, so in control, that it was almost more than she could bear, and she was consumed with boiling rage as she followed on his heels into the kitchen.

'This is *my* home, dammit,' Lexi vented furiously, 'and I want you out of it!'

Georg assessed the well-designed kitchen with one sweeping glance, then reached for the percolator, extracted a drip filter, and set about grinding the coffee beans.

Lexi viewed his back with angry vexation. '*Damn* you, don't you listen?' She reached for his arm in an attempt to drag him round to face her, and felt the sheer strength of well-honed muscle beneath her fingers.

'I heard you.' He transferred the percolator on to the element and switched it on.

'Don't you dare ignore me!'

Georg turned slowly to face her, and suddenly she was supremely conscious of his close proximity, the powerful breadth of shoulder beneath its civilised sheath of expensive tailoring.

'If you continue to behave like a belligerent child I'll treat you like one.' The words were silky-soft, and dangerous with the threat of intent.

'Oh? What particular form of punishment do you have in mind?' She was so angry that she really didn't care any more. 'Be warned that if you so much as touch me I'll have you up for assault.'

His eyes became almost black, and his mouth tightened into a thin line. Without warning he caught hold of her shoulders and drew her inextricably close. So close that she was made aware of every tautened muscle and sinew.

'Don't——'

It was far too late to bargain with him, and she cried out as his head lowered to hers, his mouth fastening with unerring accuracy over her own as he forced her tightly closed lips apart.

A silent moan failed to find voice as he initiated a brutal assault on her senses, and she struggled against him, beating her fists against his back, his ribs—anywhere she could reach.

Her jaw ached from the sheer force of his possession, and she could have screamed with frustrated rage as every attempt she made to struggle free was halted with effortless ease.

Timeless minutes later he relinquished her mouth, and she stood in shocked silence as she made a conscious effort to regain her breath, hardly aware that her face was waxen-pale and her eyes were large luminous pools mirroring a mixture of pain and disbelief.

His features appeared blurred behind the slow well of tears, and she blinked rapidly to dispel their threatened spill.

If he'd wanted to deliver a lesson in male superiority he had succeeded, although her spirit wouldn't permit him the satisfaction of knowing the depth of her shaken emotions.

Sheer unadulterated pride was responsible for the slight tilt of her chin, while a degree of dignity and self-respect lent her eyes a fiery blaze.

'If you don't leave I'll walk out of the door and book myself into a hotel for the night,' Lexi declared in a deadly calm voice.

His appraisal was swift and clinically analytical as he surveyed her beautiful features, and she hated the knowledge she glimpsed in his gaze, the sure, unabating regard that was a perplexing mixture of ruthlessness and shameless sensuality.

His eyes held hers for what seemed an age, then they slid slowly down to settle on the soft fullness of her mouth before lifting to meet her startled defiant gaze.

Then he turned and walked towards the door, opened it, and closed it quietly behind him.

Somehow she had expected him to overrule her, and, although she desperately wanted him gone, his departure was something of an anticlimax.

Damn him! She was so impossibly angry she almost wished he were still in the apartment so that she could vent some of her rage.

Except there was the pain of her ravaged mouth as a vivid reminder, and she felt a sudden chill shiver down the length of her spine in the knowledge that Georg Nicolaos would never allow himself to be subservient to any woman, much less *her*.

The frantic bubbling of the percolator penetrated her mind, and she reached forward to switch off the element, opting instead for hot milk with a generous dash of brandy.

When it was ready she carried it through to the lounge and sank into one of the large leather sofas, slipping off her shoes and nestling her feet up beneath her as she slowly sipped from the mug.

A heavy silence permeated the room, almost as if the man who had not long vacated it had left something of his presence behind, Lexi brooded as she gazed sightlessly into space.

He was everything she hated in a man, she decided with damning frustration: self-assured, arrogant, and impossibly iron-willed.

If it weren't for Jonathan she'd condemn Georg Nicolaos to the nether regions of hell without so much as a second thought.

A long heartfelt sigh escaped her lips. Five weeks, David had intimated. It would be a miracle if she survived the distance.

The brandy began to soothe her fractured nerves, and when the laced milk was finished she drifted into her bedroom, stripped off her clothes, removed her make-up, and slipped into bed to sleep deeply until seven when the alarm shrilled its loud insistent summons to the start of a new day.

CHAPTER THREE

THE photographic session went way over time, with endless extra shots being required—to such an extent that it was all Lexi could do to contain her impatience as she obediently performed for the camera.

As much as she admired Peter's professional expertise, this morning for some reason his seemingly endless search for perfection proved tiresome, and she longed for the moment he would call a halt.

'That's good, darling. Chin a fraction higher. Now turn slowly towards me. *Great*. Smile. Sultry, sexy—that's the look I want. Pout a little. Sweep down with those eyelashes. Good. Now open. Look at me.' The shutter clicked with increasing rapidity. 'That's it, darling. I've got all I need.'

With a sigh of relief Lexi stepped away from the backdrop with its concentration of lights angling in from various points on the set. The heat they generated added at least ten degrees to the temperature inside the studio, and she longed for a cool shower.

She quickly effected a change of clothes in a dressing-room at the rear of the set, and, aware of the time, Lexi simply caught up her bag and emerged to cast Peter and his two assistants a hasty grin.

'Got to dash. I'm due to model at a fashion auction at one. *Ciao*.'

It took ten minutes to reach her apartment, a further fifteen minutes to shower and dress, then she slipped back into the car and drove towards the exclusive suburb of Woollahra.

Traffic seemed unusually congested, and she managed to miss almost every set of traffic-lights at each consecutive intersection. Consequently, by the time she had parked the Mercedes she had five minutes to spare before the auction was due to begin.

Held in an exclusive boutique and organised by its owner to aid of one of Lexi's favoured charities, with guest attendance strictly by invitation, it was a twice-yearly event for which she waived her normal fee. Designer labels were displayed by three professional models and individually auctioned at a cost price reserve. Considered a 'must' by the social élite, it was definitely an occasion, with champagne and hors-d'oeuvres offered by hired staff, followed at the auction's conclusion by a sumptuous array of savouries and continental cakes served with coffee and tea.

Organised chaos reigned in the small changing-room, and Lexi murmured a quick apology as she began pulling on a pair of sheer tights.

'*Lexi*. For heaven's sake, we thought you weren't going to make it in time!'

Anxiety coloured the older woman's voice, and Lexi proffered a soothing smile. 'Relax, Renée. Jacqueline is just now beginning her welcoming introductory speech. It will be at least five minutes before she's ready to announce the first of the collection.' She stepped into a silk half-slip, then dressed in the stunning ensemble that represented an exotic and expensive line in resort wear. With skilled fingers she swept her hair up into a casually contrived knot atop her head, added adept strokes with shadow and liner to highlight her eyes, blusher to her cheeks, then outlined her mouth and brushed colour over the contour of her lips. 'There. All done.' A quick check in the mirror, a practised smile at her own reflection, then she slid her feet into slender-heeled pumps and stood waiting with poised assurance for Jacqueline's call.

Possessed of an ebullient personality and an enviable degree of showmanship, Jacqueline was very much in charge of the auction, which soon assumed the theatrics of a stage production. Without doubt she held her 'audience' in the palm of her hand, and, suitably relaxed by a generous flow of fine champagne, her guests entered into the spirit of it all with a display of friendly rivalry as they attempted to outbid each other in their race for a bargain purchase.

Elegant day-wear soon gave way to a sophisticated line of tailored business-wear, and was followed by the after-five range.

Lexi completed her walk, gave a final turn, then moved quickly into the changing-room, effecting a smooth exchange of garments with swift professional ease.

The background music was muted, a tasteful selection that didn't compete with Jacqueline's spirited auctioneering, and Lexi emerged on cue in an absolutely stunning creation that could easily have been created for her alone.

Adopting a practised smile, she moved with easy fluidity to pause, turn, then repeat the process at three-metre intervals until she'd completed the pre-arranged circuit.

As she turned to face the guests her eyes were caught by a tall figure standing on the periphery of her vision.

Georg Nicolaos. What the *hell* was he doing here?

Looking incredibly arresting in a dark business suit, his pale blue shirt worn with a sombre silk tie, he represented an alien force in what was surely a feminine sphere.

Lexi forced herself to meet his gaze and hold it for a few seconds before transferring her attention elsewhere as the bidding became fiercely competitive.

'Two hundred and fifty.'

'Four hundred.'

Heads turned as if in synchronisation at the sound of a deep masculine drawl, and Jacqueline, with immediate recognition and an impish sense of humour, broke into tinkling laughter.

'Darlings, we *are* honoured this afternoon. For those of you who haven't read this morning's papers, Georg and our darling Lexi are an item.' She paused slightly and made a delicate fluttering movement with her elegantly manicured hands. 'Don't you think it's just marvellous?' Her smile held genuine warmth as she turned towards Lexi. 'I'm so pleased for you both.' Turning back towards her guests, she lifted her hands in an expressive gesture. 'Now, ladies, is anyone going to compete with Georg?'

'Four hundred and fifty.'

'Six hundred.'

Lexi's eyes widened fractionally as she forced herself to maintain a slight smile. Inside, she could feel the onset of helpless frustration and anger at his deliberate actions.

'Seven,' followed in feminine determination.

'One thousand,' Georg drawled, lifting one eyebrow in a gesture of musing indulgence at the sound of a few gasps.

He was deliberately attempting to set a precedent in their purported relationship. His appearance here would be regarded as juicy gossip, Lexi seethed, and as such it would be discussed, embellished, and circulated with wildfire speed.

Damn him!

'Eleven hundred.'

'Twelve,' another feminine bidder added, while yet another topped it by a further two hundred dollars.

Dear lord in heaven. They were caught up with the need to outbid each other, turning a civilised event into a circus.

'Two thousand,' Georg called calmly, and there was a hushed silence.

Would anyone else dare bid? Somehow Lexi doubted it. Even the most frivolous of the women present would balk at paying three times the gown's wholesale price.

'Sold,' Jacqueline declared with a delighted clap of her hands. 'Thank you, Georg.' She turned towards Lexi and directed an ecstatic smile. 'You, too, darling.' With professional ease she commandeered her guests' attention. 'Now, ladies, please prepare yourselves for the evening-wear selection. Then I have a little surprise in store.'

Lexi escaped into the changing-room, and her fingers shook as she slid out of the gown and handed it to the assistant before donning a strapless and practically backless figure-hugging creation in patterned silk.

Any hopes she held that Georg might have made an unobtrusive exit were dashed as she re-emerged, and in silent defiance she directed him a deliberately sultry smile before veiling her eyes.

It was almost half an hour before the last evening gown was sold, and with each passing minute Lexi felt as if her nerves were being stretched to breaking point.

Georg had declined to make another bid, and his presence merely whipped speculation to fever pitch. Lexi's sensory perception was so acute that she could almost *hear* what they were thinking.

'Now, darlings, I've added an extra line as a little titillation.' Jacqueline paused, allowing her words to have maximum effect. 'What you've seen so far will certainly gain your favourite man's attention. Now, for the grand finale we'll play an ace with a range of sleep-wear guaranteed to raise his——' she hesitated with theatrical precision, then a husky voluptuous laugh escaped her lips '——blood-pressure.' From the degree of laughter filtering through to the changing-room, the guests were in fine form, their normal reserve loosened somewhat by several glasses of champagne.

Lexi cast the final rack an experienced eye, and inwardly cringed. Exclusive, ruinously expensive, the items displayed represented the finest in silk, satin and lace, and were guaranteed by the designer to be original and unduplicated.

Even attired in the exquisitely fashioned teddy, she would be just as adequately covered as if she were modelling a swim-suit. Yet there was a wealth of difference in the degree of projected provocativeness.

For a moment she considered refusing, but there were three models and consequently three of every line. If she opted out Georg, as well as every guest present, would be aware of it, and she was damned if she'd give him that satisfaction.

With professional panache she took each call, modelling first the satin lounge pyjamas, following them with a silk nightgown and négligé set in soft peach-coloured silk. The nightgown was so exquisitely designed it could easily have been worn as an evening gown, and she gave the patrons full benefit of its delightful lines by removing the négligé and completing another round.

The teddy, with an ankle-length wrap in matching satin, was left until last and presented as the *pièce de résistance*.

Lexi was the last of the three models to emerge, and she unconsciously lifted her chin a fraction higher as she moved slowly around the room, deliberately not casting so much as a glance in Georg's direction.

'Remove the wrap, darling,' Jacqueline instructed, and Lexi shook her head as she conjured forth a witching smile.

'I prefer a little mystique, Jacqueline.' The wrap had no ties, and she was careful to ensure that the lapels covered each peak of her satin-and-lace-clad breasts. Her long slim legs were beautifully smooth and lightly tanned, and with considerable grace she lifted a hand to her head, released the weight of her hair so that it cascaded in a rippling flow of thick curls down her back, then she held out the edges of her wrap and executed a slow turn before moving towards the changing-room, not caring that she was breaking with one of Jacqueline's preferred rules.

'One thousand dollars.'

No one glimpsed the flash of fury in her lovely golden eyes at the sound of that deep, faintly accented masculine voice, nor the faint tightening of her lips as she heard Jacqueline's subtle teasing and Georg's evocative drawl in response.

Instead she concentrated on changing into her own clothes, and deliberately ignored the other two models' curiosity as she re-fastened her hair into a casually elegant knot at her nape.

She would have given anything to have slipped out of the side-door and make good her escape, but Jacqueline, Lexi knew, preferred her models to mix and mingle for at least ten minutes, during which she presented each with a fashion accessory for donating their time without fee to such a worthy cause.

The social conclusion to the afternoon gave her assistants time to discreetly collect payment and distribute purchases.

Perhaps Georg had already left, Lexi decided darkly, for only the strongest man would opt to stay in a room full of animated chattering women.

She was wrong, of course. Worse, he didn't appear to be even vaguely ill at ease, and she took her time in joining him as she paused to talk with first one guest and then another as she slowly moved towards the door.

Eventually there was nowhere else for her to go, and she tilted her head slightly, centring her attention on the bridge of his aristocratic Grecian nose.

'Georg.' Her voice was a deliberately husky drawl, and she slanted one eyebrow in a gesture of teasing mockery. 'What *are* you doing here?'

His features creased into a seemingly warm, intimate smile, and his eyes were so dark it was impossible to read their expression. 'I patronise the charity organisation which benefits from this auction,' he informed her, and, lifting a hand, he casually pushed a stray tendril of hair back behind her ear. 'Knowing you were one of the models was sufficient incentive for me to put in a personal appearance.'

Dear heaven, he was good! Too damned good, she decided darkly, aware they were the focus of attention.

How had he known she'd be here this afternoon? David? As close as she was to her brother, she didn't communicate to him her every move. Therefore Georg must have deliberately sought to discover her whereabouts. The thought rankled unbearably.

'Another brilliantly calculated ploy?' Lexi arched with deliberate softness, and saw his eyes narrow fractionally.

'Five minutes,' he cautioned quietly. 'Then we'll leave.'

A slow sweet smile widened her provocatively curved mouth. 'Any longer and I won't be able to sheathe my claws.' She was so angry it was almost impossible to still the faint shakiness of her hand as she accepted a glass of chilled water from a dutiful waitress, and she kept her eyes veiled beneath long fringed lashes in an attempt to hide her true feelings.

If he so much as *dared* to present her with his purchases in front of all these women she'd be hard pressed not to throw them back at him!

A hollow laugh rose and died in her throat. It would be ironic if they weren't for her at all. No matter how much *she* hated him, there could be no doubt he was held in considerable awe by members of the opposite sex.

'You haven't forgotten we're dining with Jonathan this evening?'

Lexi spared him a level glance. 'No.' Thank heaven David would be there to act as a buffer, for sitting through an intimate family dinner would tax her acting ability to its very limit.

'News of our...relationship has reached my mother.' His eyes probed hers, seeing the faint flaring of defiance, the latent anger simmering beneath the surface of her control. 'I have been severely chastised for not having brought you to meet her.'

Her fingers tightened round the stem of her glass, and she took a steadying breath. 'I'm not sure I can stand such devotion to familial duty.'

'Lexi! *Georg!*'

It was too much to hope that they might be left alone, and Lexi had to stop herself from physically flinching as the man at her side altered his stance so that his arm pressed against her shoulder.

'Jacqueline,' he acknowledged. 'How are you?'

'Absolutely fine, darling.' Her smile was genuine, and she case Lexi a warm glance. 'You were outstanding, as always. That touch of originality at the end was quite stunning.' Her eyes lit with a hint of mischievous humour. 'Georg was suitably appreciative.'

'Overwhelmed,' he drawled in musing acknowledgment as he extracted and handed Jacqueline his cheque. 'And understandably anxious for a private encore.'

Lexi was dimly aware of Jacqueline's tinkling laughter as she proffered two gold signature-emblazoned carrier-bags.

'A lovely addition to your wardrobe, darling,' Jacqueline accorded, and, leaning forward, she brushed her lips lightly against Lexi's cheek. 'I couldn't be more delighted.'

Lexi had never felt more like screaming with vexation in her life. Yet she had to smile and pretend that Georg's gift was warmly received. The moment they were alone, she promised herself, she would verbally *slay* him.

'If you'll excuse us, Jacqueline?' Georg said smoothly.

Lexi murmured a farewell and followed it with a captivating smile, then she turned and preceded Georg from the boutique, waiting until they were on the pavement and at least ten paces from its doors before expelling a deep breath.

'You were utterly *impossible*!'

'Where are you parked?'

'Don't you *dare* ignore me!' Frustrated anger filled her voice, and, even though she pitched it low, there could be no doubt as to the extent of her fury.

'I have no intention of ignoring you,' Georg replied with deceptive calm. 'But the footpath of an exclusive shopping centre is hardly the place for a slanging match.' He directed her a look that held infinite mockery. 'Unless, of course, you have no objection to an audience of interested bystanders.'

'Where would you suggest?' she threw vengefully.

'Your apartment,' he drawled. 'After which we'll visit my mother and then join Jonathan for dinner.'

In a moment she'd erupt! 'I'm sure your mother is delightful, but I'd rather delay meeting her for a few days if you don't mind.'

'Ah, but I do mind.' He was so darned imperturbable that she felt like slapping him! 'She is expecting us at five.'

'You can call her and cancel.' Lexi walked quickly along the street in an attempt to out-pace him, and it irked her unbearably that his stride appeared leisurely by comparison.

'She is elderly and very fragile. She is also irascible, speaks her mind, and likes to have command over her children.' His voice held musing affection. 'We tend to indulge her.'

She reached the car park, and crossed to her silver Mercedes. 'Your mother may have issued a royal edict, but right now I've had about as much of you as I can stand.' She extracted her keys and unlocked the door. 'Believe that if I could opt out of dinner tonight with Jonathan, I would!' In one graceful movement she slid in behind the wheel and fired the engine.

Easing the vehicle forward, she sent it moving swiftly towards the exit without sparing so much as a glance in her rear-view mirror, and she headed towards Darling Point, uncaring as to whether he followed or not.

He really was the most insufferable, antagonistic, *frightening* man she'd ever met, Lexi fumed as she reached her apartment block and swept below street level to her allotted parking space.

Within minutes of her entering her apartment the doorbell pealed, and she flung the door open to see Georg's tall frame filling the aperture.

'How did you get past security?' she demanded instantly.

'I produced credentials, and exerted sufficient influence.' He extended two carrier-bags. 'Yours,' he declared with dangerous softness, and her eyes flared brilliantly alive with frustrated rage.

'I can't possibly accept them.'

There was a leashed quality about his stance as he entered the lounge, a silent warning evident that only a fool would choose to disregard. 'Consider them a gift.'

'For which you paid an exorbitant amount,' Lexi vented furiously, 'under the guise of a charitable donation.'

'The purchases were immaterial.'

'The main reason for your appearance at the boutique was abundantly clear,' she accorded bitterly. 'By tomorrow the society grapevine will have relayed every little detail plus embellishment and supposition.'

'Without doubt.'

Her eyes flashed. 'You don't give a damn, do you?'

He looked at her in silence, his gaze unwaveringly direct, and there was an element of ruthlessness apparent when he spoke. 'Go and get changed.'

She drew a deep, angry breath. 'I am not visiting your mother. At least, not today.'

'She's expecting us.'

He made her feel like a recalcitrant child, and she was neither. 'I don't like domineering, autocratic men who relegate women to second-class citizenship merely because of their sex.' She glimpsed a tiny flare of anger in the depths of his eyes, and chose to ignore it. 'Will you please leave? I'd like to shower and change.'

'What do you imagine I'll do if I stay?' Georg mocked cynically. 'Invade your bedroom and subject you to a display of unbridled passion?'

She managed to hold his gaze, although there was nothing she could do to prevent the soft tinge of pink that coloured her cheeks. Remembering the force of his kiss was sufficient to enable her to imagine precisely how uninhibited his lovemaking would be.

Effecting a careless shrug, she turned and walked towards the hallway, reaching her bedroom with seemingly unhurried steps where she carefully closed the door.

Damn him! Why did he ruffle her composure? Worse, why did she allow him to succeed?

Twenty minutes later she added the last touch to her make-up, then stood back from the mirror to view her image with critical assessment.

The slim-fitting dress of peacock-blue silk accentuated her slight curves, and provided a perfect foil for her dark auburn hair worn in a smooth knot at her nape with a small bow in matching blue.

Perfume, her favourite Givenchy, was sprayed to several pulse-points, then she gathered up her evening-bag and made her way to the lounge.

Georg was standing by the window, and he turned as she entered the room, his eyes conducting a sweeping appraisal that brought forth an unconscious lift of her chin as she issued coolly, 'Shall we go?'

Lexi didn't offer so much as a word as they took the lift down to street level, and she maintained an icy silence as Georg sent the Ferrari east towards Vaucluse.

As much as she wanted to rail against him, there seemed little point in continuing an argument she couldn't win.

Several butterflies inside her stomach began a series of somersaults as Georg eased the Ferrari into a wide circular driveway and brought it to a halt behind a large Mercedes.

'Relax,' he advised quietly as he slipped out from behind the wheel and moved round to open her door, and Lexi directed a brilliant smile at him as she stepped out, and walked at his side towards the imposing entrance.

'I'm perfectly relaxed,' she assured. Her eyes challenged his—wide, gold and apparently guileless.

The front door opened and they were welcomed inside by a formally suited man whose demeanour was politely deferential. 'The family are assembled in the lounge, if you would care to go through.'

Georg smiled at the butler. 'Thanks, Nathaniel.'

Lexi drew a calming breath, and drew courage from the strength of her convictions.

'Georgiou! You are late! Everyone else is here!'

A tiny figure attired entirely in black was the visual attestation of an elderly matriarch, and despite her advanced years her eyes were surprisingly alert behind gold-rimmed glasses as she sat rigidly upright in a straight-backed chair.

Lexi proffered a conciliatory smile. 'The fault is mine.'

The dark brown eyes sharpened and conducted a swift analytical assessment. 'Indeed?'

'Georg informed me less than an hour ago that you were expecting us.' Her eyebrows rose fractionally and she effected a deprecatory gesture with her hands. 'I had just finished a modelling assignment and I needed to go home and change.'

'Georgiou, are you not going to introduce this young woman to us all?'

'Of course, Mama,' Georg conceded with lazy humour. 'Lexi Harrison.'

'Lexi? What name is that?'

'My mother's favoured derivation of Alexis,' she informed her calmly, refusing to be fazed in the slightest.

'You are divorced.'

'Yes, I am.' What was this—an inquisition, for heaven's sake?

'Mama,' Georg admonished with musing indolence. 'You presume too much.'

'I agree,' a deep voice drawled, and an older version of Georg moved forward, his smile warm and welcoming. 'Lexi, how are you?'

'Alex,' Lexi acknowledged, allowing her answering smile to encompass the slim attractive-looking woman at his side.

'My wife Samantha,' he introduced. 'And this,' he paused to indicate the little girl cradled in the curve of his arm, 'is our daughter Leanne.'

'She's beautiful,' Lexi complimented, for it was true. The wide-eyed sable-haired imp was utterly adorable.

'Yes,' Alex agreed, and his eyes settled on his wife with such infinite warmth that Lexi almost caught her breath. 'I am a very fortunate man.'

'Anna and Nick are not able to be here,' Mrs Nicolaos informed them. 'Tomorrow night we will have a celebratory dinner.' Her eyes did not leave Lexi for a second. 'Precisely what do you model, young woman, and when and where did you meet Georgiou?'

The elderly woman was persistent, and 'irascible' wasn't the right word! 'Clothes,' Lexi answered with every semblance of outward calm. 'The winter, spring, summer and autumn collections of well-known designers; photographic stills for fashion magazines, and the occasional television commercial.' It wasn't in her nature to be outrageous, but the temptation to shock was irresistible. 'I don't pose in the nude, nor do I resort to the type of photography that portrays women in a state of provocative dishabille.'

Mrs Nicolaos didn't bat so much as an eyelid. 'Of course not. Your father would have disowned you.'

Lexi effected a slight moue in silent agreement. 'I met your son——'

'At a party,' Georg intervened smoothly. 'Lexi was accompanied by her brother.'

'Hmm. I do not approve of divorce.'

'Neither do I,' Lexi responded evenly. 'If I'd had any sense I would have lived in sin instead of opting for marriage. Then I could have walked away relatively unscathed.'

'And Georgiou? Do you intend walking away from him?'

This was getting worse by the minute! 'I would walk away from any man who mistreated me,' she said quietly. 'Whether he was your son or not.'

There was a palpable silence during which Lexi held the older woman's direct gaze, and for a brief moment she glimpsed a softening in those dark eyes before they moved to settle on her youngest son.

'Georgiou, open the champagne. Alexandros, relinquish my granddaughter so that she may sit with me a while.'

Leanne, who surely should have been terrified of her grandmother, ran to her side the instant Alex set her down on her feet, and the transformation on Mrs Nicolaos's face was unbelievable as Leanne caught hold of her hand. The elderly woman spoke softly in Greek, and the child gazed at her in open adoration.

'She's a darling,' Samantha said gently, interpreting Lexi's glance. 'She also guards her family like a lioness. If it's any consolation, she attempted to tear me apart the first time Alex brought me here.'

'Champagne,' Georg announced, handing Samantha and Lexi each a slim crystal flute, while Alex crossed to his mother's side.

'Sit down. Why is everyone standing?' Mrs Nicolaos demanded, directing both Alex and Georg a fierce look.

'Out of deference to you, Mama,' Alex declared gently. 'If it pleases you for us to be seated, then we shall do so for a short while. Then we will leave, and you must rest.'

'Bah! I am not an invalid!'

'You are infinitely precious to us all. That is why our visits are designed not to overtax your strength.' Alex leaned forward and brushed his lips against the lined cheek. 'Now, shall we have our champagne?'

It was almost six when they made their farewells, and, seated in the Ferrari, Lexi leaned back against the head-rest as Georg fired the engine and eased the car down the driveway behind Alex's Mercedes.

'You didn't tell me it was going to be the Nicolaos family *en masse*,' she berated him the instant the car entered the street.

He gave her a dark, penetrating glance before returning his attention to the road. 'Does it matter that Alex and Samantha were there?'

'This whole thing is beginning to getting out of hand,' she retaliated, hating the degree of deception involved. In the beginning it had seemed relatively uncomplicated, and now she wasn't so sure.

'Yet you were aware when you agreed that it was all or nothing,' Georg reminded her silkily.

'At the time I had little conception of what "all" would involve,' Lexi opined drily.

Only a few blocks separated his mother's home from Jonathan's exclusive residence, and they reached the elegant tudor-styled mansion in less than five minutes.

David's Ferrari was nowhere in sight, and Lexi wasn't sure whether to be relieved or disappointed at being the first to arrive.

'Before we go inside I suggest you slip this on.'

'This' was a brilliant square diamond set on a slender gold band, and she looked at him in consternation. 'You can't be serious?'

'Very.'

'Don't you think it's taking things a bit too far?'

'If we've been keeping our affair under wraps until your divorce was finalised, now that we've gone public surely the next logical step is a formal announcement of our forthcoming marriage?'

'No.'

'You don't think Jonathan will rest easy until he has proof that my intentions are honourable?'

Her eyes glittered with unspoken rage as he calmly slid the ring on to her finger. 'Damn you,' she accorded bitterly.

'Shall we go in?' There was an edge of mockery apparent. 'I imagine Sophie has heard us arrive, and your father will be curious as to why we're taking so long.'

CHAPTER FOUR

JONATHAN greeted them at the door, and Lexi returned his affectionate embrace with enthusiasm, smiling as he put her at arm's length.

'Come inside. I thought we'd relax out on the terrace. David will be delayed by about ten minutes, and Sophie has organised dinner for six-thirty.'

Home. The house where she had grown up, she mused as she followed Jonathan indoors. It was amazing how secure she felt within these walls, how protected.

It took only a few minutes for him to notice the significance of the ring on her finger. His pleasure brought her close to tears, and she could hardly protest when he brought out a bottle of Dom Perignon to celebrate the occasion.

'I'm delighted to have you both as my guests.'

The genuineness of her father's enthusiasm couldn't be doubted, and Lexi managed a suitable smile in response.

Georg, damn him, stayed close to her side, and even David's arrival did little to diminish his attention.

The warmth of his smile appeared so honest it was all she could do not to reel from its impact, and she was forced to suffer the touch of his hand on her elbow as he led her into dinner.

Sophie served the first course, a delicious beef consommé, and followed it with deep-fried prawns in a nest of finely shredded lettuce. The main course was a superb duck *à l'orange* with tiny roast potatoes, honeyed carrots, courgettes and beans.

David took care to ensure that the appropriate wine accompanied each course, although Lexi sipped at the contents of her glass and declined to have it refilled, opting for chilled water instead.

Conversation flowed, touching on a variety of subjects that pertained primarily to business and mutual acquaintances, and to all intents and purposes it appeared to be a convivial family gathering.

It proved, Lexi perceived a trifle wryly, what excellent actors they were.

'When do you go into hospital, Daddy?' It was a question she had to ask, and there was nothing she could do to mask her anxiety.

'Sunday week, darling,' Jonathan revealed gently. 'Surgery is scheduled for the following day.'

'You've always been so careful, eating the right foods, not smoking, exercising each day. I can't believe something like this could happen to you.'

'Let's admit it, Father is a human dynamo,' David declared with a slow smile. 'Always accepting a new challenge, fighting to make it succeed. Continually pitting his wits against unforeseen obstacles.'

Lexi captured her father's eyes and held them with her own. 'I think you'd better re-evaluate your life and slow down.' Without thought, she added with a light laugh, 'I want you around to appreciate your grandchildren.'

'Indeed,' Georg acceded with musing enthusiasm, and there was nothing Lexi could do in protest as he lifted her hand to his lips to kiss each finger in turn—a deliberately blatant gesture that taxed all her strength not to snatch her hand from his grasp.

'Grandchildren,' Jonathan repeated bemusedly. 'I like that idea.'

'You'll forgive me if I agree,' Georg declared with a husky chuckle, leaving no one in any doubt just where his thoughts lay.

Lexi reached out and deliberately traced the tip of her highly polished fingernail across the back of his left hand as she directed him a brilliantly warm smile. 'Steady, darling. I've only just accepted your engagement ring.'

As if sensing her protest Georg lifted a hand and his gaze was infinitely disturbed as he touched a finger to her lips. 'Something which has made me a very happy man.'

She wanted to *kill* him. Yet all she could do was smile.

'Have you made any plans for the wedding?'

'We thought a quiet affair, confined to family and close friends. Five weeks from now,' Georg indicated, and, on hearing Lexi's slightly audible gasp, he leant forward and bestowed a fleeting kiss on her as she opened her mouth to protest. 'If I had my way we'd obtain a special licence and marry within a matter of days.'

How could he sit there and announce such a thing? Lexi was so utterly furious that it was a wonder she didn't erupt with rage.

He turned towards Jonathan, totally ignoring her. 'That will give you time to recuperate sufficiently from surgery. Are you happy to leave all the arrangements to me?'

Her father couldn't have looked more delighted. 'Of course. I can't begin to tell you both how happy this makes me. Now I can enter hospital with a clear mind, knowing that if anything happens Lexi will be taken care of by someone who has my utmost respect.'

Oh, dear lord! After such fulsome enthusiasm how could she possibly refute it? Lexi groaned with frustration. But how far did it have to go? Surely specific arrangements for a wedding were hardly necessary?

'A church wedding, darling?'

'I don't think so, Daddy,' she negated quietly. 'I had all that before.' She lifted a hand and smoothed back a stray tendril of hair in a purely defensive gesture.

'The gardens are lovely—so colourful at this time of year,' Jonathan enthused. 'Would you consider marrying at home?'

'A marvellous idea,' Georg conceded, slanting Lexi such a warm glance that she almost reeled from its implied intimacy. 'Early afternoon? Followed by champagne and hors-d'oeuvres. Unless there is any objection, I would prefer the reception to be held in the restaurant. It is regarded as something of a family tradition, and would give my mother immense pleasure.'

The tension robbed her of her appetite, and she declined dessert and the cheeseboard, and opted instead for coffee laced with liqueur and cream.

Consequently her nerves had tightened almost to breaking point by the time they took their leave.

'Take good care of Lexi for me,' Jonathan bade Georg as he escorted them to the door.

'I fully intend to,' Georg declared with quiet emphasis, and Lexi was forced to suffer his arm about her waist as he led her down to the car.

Almost as soon as they were clear of the driveway she burst into angry, voluble speech.

'Did you *have* to be so——' she paused as words momentarily failed her '—proprietorial?' Her fingers clenched until the knuckles showed white as she gripped the clasp of her evening-bag. 'You sat there so damned *calmly*, looking at me as if . . .' She trailed to a frustrated halt, loath to say what Georg had no compunction in voicing.

'I couldn't wait to get you home and into bed?' he completed in a drawling tone, adding with cynical mockery, 'Is it so surprising that I might want to?'

'Discussing a wedding and prospective grand-children!' Outrage brought her anger to boiling point. 'It was totally ridiculous!'

'If I remember correctly, it was you who brought up the subject of grandchildren,' he alluded in droll tones, and she clenched her hands in an effort not to physically *hit* him!

'What on earth do you think you're *doing*, for heaven's sake?'

'Driving you home.'

An impossible fury rose within. 'Don't be facetious!'

'We'll discuss it rationally over coffee.'

'You're being deliberately evasive, skilfully utilising boardroom tactics to avoid the issue!' she accused heatedly.

'I am merely attempting to defuse your temper sufficiently until I'm in a position to satisfactorily deal with it.'

'Don't you dare patronise me. I won't stand for it!'

He didn't respond, and she sat in angry silence for several seconds before turning towards him. 'Stop the car. I'll hail a taxi.' She was so incensed that she reached for the door-handle without even caring that the car was travelling along the main arterial road towards Rose Bay.

'Don't be a fool!'

His words were harsh, demanding obedience, and she instinctively braced her body as he brought the Ferrari to a smooth halt alongside the kerb.

The handle refused to function, and she pulled at it fruitlessly for a number of seconds before becoming aware that he'd activated the locking mechanism.

'Release it, damn you!'

'I will, when you've calmed down,' Georg voiced implacably, switching off the engine and turning sideways to face her.

Incensed almost beyond endurance, she turned and lashed out at him, an action that was swiftly stilled as he caught hold of her hands and held them in a bone-crushing grip.

'You unspeakable fiend!' Topaz eyes glittered with fury as she made a futile attempt to break free.

His hands tightened, and she cried out in pain. 'You'll only succeed in hurting yourself.'

Part of her was appalled by the enormity of her actions while the other deplored the extent of her behaviour. 'Then let me go.'

His hard, intent stare played havoc with her nerve-ends, and she stifled a silent scream at the strength of purpose in those chilling depths. 'Your hands, yes,' he agreed, relinquishing them, and she rubbed them to ease the bruised bones.

She felt like a steel rope that had been rendered taut almost to breaking point. At any second she was in danger of snapping. Her mouth quivered as she drew a deep calming breath, and her hands shook uncontrollably.

'Perhaps you would care to tell me why you react so violently at the thought that a man might want to make love to you?'

Her thoughts scattered into a deep dark void where she couldn't retrieve them, and she stared blankly out of the windscreen, unable to summon her voice through the physical lump that had risen in her throat.

No one, not even Jonathan—dear lord, especially not Jonathan—knew just how deep were the scars from her association with Paul. The night she'd left him would be indelibly imprinted in her brain for as long as she lived. The explosive argument, one of many they'd had over money, had resulted in her expressing an intention to leave him and had ended in physical abuse of the worst kind. Paul had forced her to submit to sex, and afterwards she'd simply pulled on some clothes and ordered a taxi to take her to a motel. The next day she'd rung Jonathan and David and told them the marriage was over.

Lexi had little idea of the passage of time. It could have been five minutes or fifteen; she retained no recollection. At last she moved her head slightly, and her pale profile stood out in sharp contrast against the night's darkness.

'There's a beach not far from here. I'd like to walk for a while.'

Her voice sounded strangely quiet, almost dis-embodied, and she wasn't conscious of him reaching for the ignition until she heard the refined purr of the engine.

She sat in silence as he traversed the distance then pulled to a halt alongside a short flight of steps leading down on to the sandy foreshore.

Georg slid out from behind the wheel and walked round to open her door, watching with narrowed eyes as she slipped off her shoes.

He followed her actions, pushing the elegant hand-crafted imported shoes on to the floor before bending low to turn up the cuffs of his trousers. Then he straightened and locked the car, taking care to activate the alarm before moving to the head of the steps where he stood, impossibly tall and vaguely forbidding, silhouetted against the skyline.

The stretch of beach appeared deserted, and she longed for solitude. 'I can walk on my own.'

'I go with you, or you don't go at all,' Georg declared inflexibly.

Without a further word she moved past him, and, once down on the sand, she wandered out towards the gentle out-going tide, then began following its edge as the bay curved towards an outcrop of rocks.

There was a faint breeze, and she felt it tease loose a few strands of hair so that they brushed against her face.

The sand was wet beneath her bare feet, and there was just the soft sound of water lapping gently against the distant rocks. Every now and then a car sped past on the road, but the noise was far enough away not to intrude.

Somehow she expected Georg to attempt conversation, but he walked at her side in silence, and she was grateful for his perception.

On reaching the rocks, they turned as if by tacit agreement and began retracing their steps. Lexi felt the cool air on her face, and in an unbidden gesture she lifted her hand to her hair and freed the knot so that its length fell down her shoulders.

A sense of peace invaded her being, rather like the calm after a storm, and she tried to tell herself that it had nothing to do with the man at her side.

Instinct warned her that he was someone she would infinitely prefer to have as a friend than an enemy, for in opposition he'd prove a formidable force.

A slight shiver shook her slim frame, although it had nothing to do with feeling cold, and she gave a start of surprise when he shrugged off his jacket and placed it around her shoulders.

His fingers brushed her nape as he lifted her hair free, and Lexi spared him a quick glance, unable to read anything from his expression, and her murmured thanks sounded indistinct on the night air.

For some strange reason she felt as if she'd been enveloped in a security blanket, and she wasn't sure whether to feel alarmed or relieved.

The smooth jacket-lining was silky against her skin, and still held the warmth from his body. It was far too big for her, and its weight brought an awareness of his height and breadth. Evident, too, was the clean smell of the fine woollen material and the elusive woody tones of his cologne.

They reached the short flight of steps leading up on to the road far too quickly, and after dusting sand from their feet they each retrieved their shoes prior to sliding into the car.

Within a matter of minutes the Ferrari drew to a halt in the courtyard adjoining her apartment block, and she was powerless to prevent him from following her indoors.

Any argument seemed futile, and she simply extracted her key while they took the lift to her designated floor.

'Coffee?'

Lexi closed her eyes, then slowly opened them again in utter frustration. 'If you want coffee, *you* make it!'

He took the key from her fingers and unlocked the door, then he pushed her gently inside. 'I fully intend to,' he drawled. 'I merely asked if you would like some.'

'Oh—go to hell!'

His eyes speared hers, dark and fathoms deep with the silent threat of an emotion she didn't even begin to comprehend. 'Believe that I could take you there, and you would hate every second of it.'

Her whole body froze in seemingly slow motion, and her eyes became wide as they assumed a haunted, hunted quality. A glaze seemed to dull their expression as she stared sightlessly ahead, oblivious to her surroundings, the man a few feet distant—*everything* except a vivid event that would never be erased from her memory.

When he lifted a hand towards her she visibly flinched and averted her head to one side, instinctively shielding her face with her hands, and therefore missing the brief hardness that flared in his eyes.

'Cristos!' The harsh, softly husked oath sounded savage in the silence of the room, but it barely registered. He made a compulsive movement, then checked it as he demanded in a dangerously soft voice, 'Did Paul *hit* you?'

She blinked slowly, and the glaze gradually dissipated. A shiver shook her slender frame, and she hugged her arms together across her breasts in an attempt to contain it.

'Answer me, Lexi.'

The quietness of his voice didn't deceive her, and she stood, hesitant, loath to resurrect that fateful night.

'Yes.'

'Nothing more?'

She looked at him fearlessly as the silence between them became a palpable entity. Her breath hurt in her throat, constricting it almost beyond the ability to speak. 'Does it matter?'

She sensed his inner rage as he murmured something viciously explicit in his own language, and her chin lifted in an unbidden gesture as she sought a measure of strength.

'I think I'd like that coffee,' she indicated, meeting his compelling gaze with courage and dignity.

Georg's stance didn't alter for several heart-stopping seconds, then he turned and made his way towards the kitchen.

When he returned he placed a tall handled glass into her hands. 'Drink all of it.'

Lexi tasted the contents, and effected a faint grimace in recognition of the measure of brandy he'd added to the cream-topped brew. She almost never touched spirits, and it was more than a year since she'd had to resort to taking the occasional sleeping-pill. Obediently she sipped until the glass was empty, then set it down on a nearby table.

'Would you mind leaving now? It's late, and I'd like to go to bed.'

He slowly drained his glass, then held it between his hands. 'Have lunch with me tomorrow.'

'Today,' Lexi corrected absently. 'And no, I think I'd rather be alone.' The beginnings of a faint smile tugged one edge of her mouth. 'We're dining with your mother. I'll need to harness all my resources.'

'My family is not in the least formidable.'

She moved towards the lobby, and paused by the front door. 'That's a matter of opinion.'

Gentle fingers lifted her chin, and her lashes swiftly lowered as she felt his fingertips trace the outline of her mouth. Beneath his feather-light touch she was unable to control the slight trembling, and she stood very still as he brushed his lips against her temple.

'Be ready at six.'

As soon as he had gone she locked up and moved back into the lounge, activating the television set in a bid to discover a programme that would catch her interest until exhaustion set in and provided an escape into oblivion.

CHAPTER FIVE

Lexi chose to wear a stunning gown in emerald-green silk, its smooth lines hugging the delicate curves of her breasts, her waist, then flaring out from the hips to fall in generous folds to calf-length. Matching shoes and evening-bag completed the outfit, and her make-up was deliberately understated. In a last-minute decision she opted to leave her hair loose, using side-clips to hold its thick length away from her face.

The doorbell chimed just as she emerged into the lounge, and she moved quickly towards the lobby to answer its summons.

Georg stood framed in the aperture, attired in an immaculate dark suit and white linen shirt, and exuding a combination of dynamic masculinity and raw virility. 'Punctuality is one of your virtues,' he greeted her with a slow disturbing smile, and Lexi effected a faint shrug.

'Not always. Shall we leave?'

George headed the Ferrari towards Double Bay and slid to a halt adjacent to the shopping centre.

'Why are you stopping here?'

'Quite simply because this is where we're dining.'

'The restaurant? I thought we were dining with your mother,' Lexi said, faintly perplexed at the change in plan.

'Mama suggested that we celebrate according to Greek tradition,' Georg informed her smoothly. 'So tonight the restaurant is closed to all but family and close friends.'

'A party?'

'Specifically to celebrate our forthcoming marriage.'

She felt the nerves in her stomach clench in painful rejection. 'This entire débâcle gets worse with every passing day,' she opined wretchedly.

His appraisal was swiftly analytical as he raked her slim form. 'Relax.'

'How can I relax?' she retorted. 'Your family and friends will examine and dissect my every word as they attempt to determine whether I'm worthy of acceptance into the Nicolaos clan.'

'There can be no doubt that they will approve my choice,' he mocked, and she gave a short laugh.

'No one would dare oppose you.'

'You do,' he drawled.

'Only because you have the ability to make me impossibly angry!'

'We're almost there,' Georg declared imperturbably.

'And it's smile-time,' she said with a trace of bitterness.'

'You do it so well.'

'Oh, stop being so damned cynical!' She was almost at the end of her tether, and being faced with the prospect of a celebratory party where they would be the focus of attention was almost more than she could bear.

Yet somehow she managed to portray a combination of gracious sincerity and suitable bewitchment with the youngest Nicolaos son.

There was a variety of food to tempt the most critical palate, and sufficient of it to feed an army. Beneath Georg's persuasive touch, Lexi sampled several delicacies and followed it with a light white wine.

At times she thought she was a little over the top, and Georg merely compounded the situation by playing the part of adoring lover to the hilt.

Her ring was admired and commented upon, and inevitably the question arose as to a possible wedding date.

'The end of January,' Georg revealed, and laughed softly at Lexi's obvious surprise. 'Do you blame me? I have no intention of allowing her to slip through my fingers.'

'And the honeymoon?'

'Greece. Where else?'

Where else, indeed?

'Are you *mad*?' Lexi demanded in a subdued voice the instant they had a moment alone. To any onlookers they must appear a loving couple, drifting close together on the dance-floor. Bouzoukis played softly in the background a haunting melody that seemed filled with pathos, as were many of the Greek songs.

'All of these people are very dear friends,' Georg murmured close to her ear.

'There can be no mistake that they imagine this to be an engagement party.' She was so angry that her whole body shook with it. 'They've brought gifts, which will have to be returned. And why did you have to give out a wedding date?'

'In a few minutes the music will change. The women will sit at the tables and watch as the men take to the floor and dance.'

Lexi looked at him with helpless frustration. 'Including you?'

'Especially me,' he informed cynically, 'in an attempt to convince everyone I am a strong virile man who will promise his prospective wife many fine sons to carry the Nicolaos name.'

'The dance is a feat of strength?'

'Symbolic endurance,' George drawled, and his dark eyes gleamed with amusement as twin flags of colour stained her cheeks. 'Come, you will sit with my mother, Anna and Samantha.'

'I'll probably walk straight out the door.'

'Be sure that I will follow and drag you back.'

The threat of his intent was without doubt, and, unbidden, her eyes moved to rest on the sensual curve of his mouth, widening slightly and assuming momentary vulnerability in memory of the havoc he'd wrought the previous evening.

His gaze narrowed, then he lowered his head down to hers.

No one could possibly have heard what they were saying, and there wasn't one guest present who doubted the reason behind the brief seemingly passionate kiss the prospective bridegroom bestowed on his bride-to-be in the middle of the dance-floor before leading her to sit in the bosom of his family as the music assumed a traditional slow lilting beat.

Lexi sat perfectly still, a smile fixed permanently in place, as each of the men removed their jackets and rolled back their shirt-sleeves before taking up their positions on the dance-floor.

Together, with arms outstretched and in perfect unison, they began to move in time to the music, their steps quickening as the beat slowly increased, until only the very fit were able to sustain the rapid tempo.

Alex and Anna's husband Nick remained with Georg, as well as a few of the younger men, and Lexi found herself unconsciously holding her breath as the impossible beat continued.

There was a crash of broken crockery as a plate hit the wooden floor, quickly followed by another, until it was difficult to distinguish the sound of each plate.

'Lexi. Here is one for you.'

Turning, she saw the proffered plate extended in Samantha's hand.

'Throw it as a gesture of appreciation.'

'You're joking.'

'It will be noticed if you don't,' Samantha cautioned softly. 'By everyone.'

'Greek tradition?'

A mischievous smile lit Samantha's beautiful features. 'Feminine enthusiasm.'

Taking the plate, Lexi looked at Georg and calmly threw it on to the floor. For her it was a gesture of suppressed anger, and, without thinking, she picked up another for good measure and sent it following in the path of the first.

It was only when she had another plate pressed into her hand that she realised the significance of the numbers thrown.

Georg, damn him, merely laughed, his dark eyes alive with devilish humour, and Lexi wanted to curl up and die as Mrs Nicolaos took up a plate and extended it.

To refuse would have been incredibly rude, and, forcing a smile, she took it and sent it crashing to the floor.

'Well done,' Samantha accorded softly. 'You've now been officially accepted into the family.'

The music reached a crescendo, then abruptly stopped, and Lexi soon saw why as several waiters with brooms appeared and began clearing up the debris, while the men had glasses of wine pressed into their hands to quench their thirst.

It wasn't long before the bouzoukis were taken up again, and this time the men fetched their womenfolk on to the dance-floor.

Georg's skin felt warm beneath her fingers, his arms hard with corded muscle, and there was nothing Lexi could do to prevent being held close in against his body. She could feel the powerful beat of his heart, and sense the musky aroma of his cologne.

'Soon Alex and Samantha will take Mama home, then gradually everyone will leave,' Georg informed her as he led her among the dancing couples.

'Your mother is amazing,' she told him.

'Be sure that she has rested all day, and tomorrow will not be permitted to rise from her bed.'

'You're extremely protective of her.'

'Mama is a very special woman,' he accorded quietly. 'Her husband, his dreams; the children, and now the grandchildren. Together they have been her reason for living.' She sensed his faint smile. 'You have her approval.'

'Should I feel flattered?'

'Without question.'

'I wonder why,' Lexi mused. 'Could it be because I stand up for myself, and don't pretend you're God and any number of sacred saints all rolled into one?'

He slanted her a wry look that was tempered with humour. 'Perhaps she sees, as I do, a girl whose inner beauty surpasses her physical attributes.'

The breath caught in her throat. 'I don't think either of you knows me well enough to reach an adequate conclusion.'

'No?'

She felt defeated, and stiffened slightly as his lips brushed her temple. 'Please don't.'

'What a contrary combination of words,' Georg mocked. 'The first encourages, while the second is a refusal.'

'Perhaps I unconsciously chose them because I am a contrary creature!'

Gently he withdrew his arms, and her eyes reflected the sudden loss of security before she successfully masked their expression. 'Alex is about to leave with Mama,' he informed. 'Come, we will bid them goodnight, then stand together and thank our guests as they leave.'

It was an hour before they were able to get away, and in the car Lexi simply leaned well back and let her head sink against the head-rest. As Georg fired the engine, she closed her eyes, and didn't open them until he brought the car to a standstill outside the entrance to her apartment block.

'There's no need for you to come in.'

'Nevertheless, I will see you safely indoors.'

It was far too late to protest, and she was overcome with helpless frustration as she passed through the entrance lobby *en route* to the lifts.

'Don't you ever *listen*?' she burst out scant minutes later as he withdrew her set of keys, selected one and inserted it into the lock of her apartment.

'Always.'

'Then why are you *here*?'

He took time to close the door carefully before turning back to face her. 'Would you believe— because I want to be?'

Lexi closed her eyes, then slowly opened them again. 'Doesn't it matter that *I* don't want you here?'

He reached forward and brushed his fingers lightly along the edge of her jaw, then slipped to cup her chin. 'Precisely what are you afraid of?' Georg queried with cynical mockery, and her eyes assumed the hue of brilliant gold.

'Will you please leave? I'm tired and I want to go to bed.'

'Are you working tomorrow?'

'No. I intend sleeping in, then taking a picnic lunch to the beach, where I can enjoy a few hours of uninterrupted solitude.'

'In preparation for the party we're to attend tomorrow evening,' he drawled, and, leaning forward, he kissed her on the mouth, a hard, passionate possession that left her wide-eyed and faintly hurt. 'Sweet dreams, Lexi.'

Then he turned and left, closing the door quietly behind him.

*   *   *

Lexi chose a beach more than an hour's drive north of the city, and, with Christmas only a matter of days away, there were very few people electing to spend valuable shopping time lazing on a sandy foreshore.

For a number of hours she simply stretched out beneath the shade of a beach umbrella and read a thick paperback, then she applied a liberal dose of sunscreen and cautiously exposed herself to the sun's rays for a short space of time.

At four she packed everything into the boot of the Mercedes and drove back to Darling Point, where she showered and shampooed her hair in preparation for the evening ahead.

The party was a perfectly splendid affair, Lexi mused as she stood with apparent ease at Georg's side in a sumptuously appointed lounge of a harbourside mansion noted for being one of the city's finest. The guests numbered among the social élite, and each of the women appeared to have spent several hours, if not the entire day, on their appearance, so exquisitely perfect were their hairstyles and make-up. Collectively their designer clothes would have cost a small fortune, and a king's ransom was represented in jewellery.

She took a small sip of an innocuously mild spritzer, then gave a faint start of surprise as she saw Anaïs Pembleton moving determinedly towards them.

'Lexi, *darling*, how are you?' Without pausing for breath, the society matron greeted Georg. 'I'm so pleased you've managed to persuade this beautiful, beautiful girl back on to the social scene.'

'Anaïs,' Georg acknowledged, his expression politely bland.

'Congratulations are in order, I hear. May one ask when the wedding is to take place?'

'Oh, there's no hurry,' Lexi hastened to reply swiftly, only to be caught by Georg's look of musing indulgence.

'I am not a patient man,' he offered with a warm smile. 'If I had my way it would be tomorrow.'

Lexi seethed in silence, angry beyond belief at Georg's deliberate ploy. The sound of the society matron's laughter was the living end, and she gave into temptation and uttered sweetly, 'You know what they say about "once bitten, twice shy".'

'Oh, yes, darling. But this time, surely it's different?' The emphasis was there, and it succeeded in rousing her temper almost to boiling point. 'I mean, Georg is impossibly rich, whereas Paul...'

There was a faint pause, and Lexi finished with seeming sweetness, 'Was a Lothario and a leech?' Her eyes contained a dangerous sparkle. 'Why not say it to my face, Anaïs? It's no secret that it's been said behind my back.'

There was a faint gasp, then the older woman drew herself up to her full height as she mentally bore down on the slim young girl facing up to her with far more courage than she'd ever imagined possible. 'My dear Lexi,' she purred softly, 'you're surely not accusing me of anything?'

Lexi's smile was the epitome of innocence. 'Now why should you imagine that?'

'I am no rumour-monger,' Anaïs Pembleton assured with chilling hauteur.

'Merely a purveyor of purported fact.' Lexi attempted to defuse the strength of her stinging words with a solemn and faintly sad smile. 'If you'll excuse me, I really must powder my nose.' There was no need for any part of her exquisitely made-up features to be retouched, but if she didn't escape now she'd end up saying something totally regrettable.

The powder-room was empty, and Lexi withdrew several tissues, dampened them, then pressed the refreshingly cool pads against both temples before standing back to examine her features.

Her eyes looked incredibly large and luminous, and there were twin flags of colour high on each cheekbone. Her mouth looked far too full. Luscious, she decided, twisting the curved edges into an expression of self-derision.

She possessed the kind of looks most girls would have killed for, and a figure that was the envy of any self-respecting female. Nature, she accorded, had certainly been extremely gracious in her endowment. Add a successful career, bankability, considerable assets, and it all added up to something that was almost too good to be true.

On an impulse she lifted her hands and tore out the restraining pins from her hair, letting its length cascade down her back in a glorious thick mass of curls.

Gone was the slender-necked society belle with her air of fragility, for now Lexi resembled a contender in the promiscuity stakes.

A quirk of amusement lifted the edge of her lips. It was amazing what a different hairstyle and a change in expression could do! It remained to be seen whether Georg would appreciate the difference.

There was a gleam of defiance in her eyes as she entered the lounge, and she saw him at once, standing tall in a group of elegantly suited men.

It was marvellous how men gravitated towards each other on the pretext of discussing business. Jonathan was a prime example, as was David.

Perhaps it was time to give Georg a taste of his own medicine. A social occasion was meant to be exactly that—social, she determined, as she threaded her way through the guests to where he stood. And *she* could play charades equally as well as he could!

Deep in conversation, he turned slightly, then his gaze narrowed fractionally as he caught sight of her.

'Darling,' Lexi greeted, a deceptively soft smile parting her mouth as she placed fingers on the sleeve of his jacket. 'I'm dying of thirst.' Her eyes were wide and deep as she gazed up at him. 'Would you mind getting me another drink?'

'Of course,' Georg acceded as he excused himself from the group. 'Wine, or something stronger?'

'Stronger, definitely.'

'That bad?' he quizzed lightly. 'You sound as if you're planning an escape.'

Her lashes swept high and wide, and she attempted a singularly sweet smile. 'Only cowards cut and run, and I won't allow Anaïs Pembleton the pleasure.'

His gleaming gaze did strange things to her equilibrium. 'Then why not forgo the drink, and we'll drift out on to the terrace and dance?'

Lexi swallowed the sudden lump that had risen in her throat. 'No, I don't think so.'

'Afraid, *darling*?'

Her chin lifted fractionally. 'Of you, Georg?' She tilted her head slightly in the pretence of examining his features. 'You're so shockingly powerful, one derives the impression you have only to blink and the markets tremble. Yet I don't fear you.'

'Perhaps you should.'

Her eyes didn't waver. 'If you don't want to fetch me a drink I'll get one myself.'

Without a word he moved towards the bar, and returned with a vodka and orange juice.

'Did Jonathan never spank you as a child?' he queried mildly as she took the glass from his hand.

'He never had to,' Lexi retorted swiftly.

His mouth curved into a musing smile. 'The perfect juvenile, hmm? Picture-book pretty, with a complexion like porcelain, and impossibly long auburn hair bound in plaits.'

'Talk to David. He'll tell you I walked in his shadow, always wanting to play.'

'Did he allow you to?'

'Most of the time,' she answered, quietly reflective, yet her voice held a tinge of wryness. 'All his friends thought I was cute, and I survived puberty without braces or acne.'

'Is it such a handicap being beautiful?' he queried with soft cynicism, and she shot him a dark pensive glance.

'Sometimes I could scream for people to see beyond the façade, to be liked for *me*, everything that is Alexis Honore Harrison. Not simply Jonathan Harrison's daughter, or David Harrison's sister. Or even Lexi Harrison, model.' She effected a helpless shrug. 'There was a time when I thought of hiring a four-wheel drive and travelling north to Kakadu Reserve,' she continued broodingly as she sipped from her glass.

'Tracking kangaroos and crocodiles, dressed in khaki and wearing an akubra hat?' He lifted a hand and touched the tip of his forefinger to the edge of her nose. 'Living life in the rough and exposing this beautiful skin to the heat and dust and other unmentionable elements.' His finger slid down to the curve of her upper lip, then gently traced its outline. 'The trouble with running away is that eventually you have to return. And the problems you wanted to escape from still remain. It's better to stay and deal with them.' His smile was warm and completely disarming. 'Believe me.'

It was impossible to still the faint trembling of her mouth. 'You sound like Jonathan and David.'

He reached out and caught her arm in a light clasp. 'Come out on to the terrace. It's cooler, and we can talk without half the room watching our every move.'

He was weaving a subtle magical spell, and the crazy thing was that she drew great comfort from the touch of his hand. It was almost as if he represented a large stable rock to which she could cling, and be safe from the storm-tossed sea threatening to engulf her. Yet that in itself was a parody, for Georg Nicolaos represented a far bigger threat than she'd ever encountered, and she wasn't sure precisely how she was going to deal with it.

He was right, she accorded a few minutes later. The terrace was cooler, and it was nothing less than sheer bliss to be free of the surreptitious glances and the mild exasperation of knowing she was the subject of conjecture.

'Shall we dance?'

'Must we?'

He took the glass from her hand and placed it down on the wide ledge of the balustrading. 'I think so. I shan't bite,' he drawled with hateful mockery, and she stiffened as he drew her close.

'If you even dared,' Lexi warned with soft vehemence, 'I'd——'

'What? Bite me back?'

Damn him, he was amused! *'Yes!'*

'I'm almost tempted. The result could prove——' he paused deliberately '—interesting, shall we say?'

He held her impossibly close, and she felt consumed with futile anger. 'Damn you!' she burst out in a furious undertone. 'This isn't dancing!'

'Why not relax?' Georg queried imperturbably, restraining her efforts to wrest herself free with galling ease.

'The only way I can relax is when I'm ten feet away from you!' she declared vehemently.

'That's quite an admission. Have you stopped to consider why?'

His silky drawl was the very limit, and her head reared back as she sought to deliver a bitter invective. Except that the words never found voice as his mouth closed over hers in a kiss that took all her fine anger and tamed it into subdued submission.

'Don't ever do that again,' Lexi said shakily several long seconds after he'd relinquished her mouth. That long, infinitely slow possession had been one of the most evocative, erotic experiences of her life. Eyes closed, she had wanted it to go on and on, and never stop. And she'd wanted so much more than just the mere coupling of their mouths.

For the first time since those initial heady days with Paul she wanted, *needed* a complete satiation of the senses that went way beyond mere seduction. Not just with any man. *This* man, a tiny voice taunted.

And he knew. It was there in his eyes, the soft curve of his mouth, the possessiveness of his hands as they moved lightly down her back to curve her close against the hard length of his body.

She unconsciously pleaded with him, her eyes large luminous pools that shimmered with the threat of crystalline tears. 'Let me go.'

His gaze darkened fractionally, and his mouth moved to form a sensual curve. 'What if I refuse?'

She felt as if she were caught up in a swirling vortex of emotion so treacherous that she was in danger of drowning. 'Please.' The effort it cost her to summon a faint smile was beyond measure. 'I——' she hesitated, and her lips trembled slightly as her eyes silently beseeched him '—I don't want to play this particular game.'

His head lowered, and his lips brushed the length of her jaw to settle at the corner of her mouth. 'Who said it was a game?'

A single tear overflowed and slowly trickled down her cheek. 'You're not playing fair.'

'That depends on your definition of the word.'

If she didn't attempt to instil some levity into the situation she'd fragment into a thousand pieces. 'Shall we go back indoors?'

He lifted his head. 'Do you particularly want to?'

'I think so,' she said steadily. 'We've stayed out here sufficiently long to make our absence convincing.'

His eyes gleamed darkly in the shadowy light. 'One look at you will be enough to convince anyone,' he mocked gently as he lifted a hand and smoothed back a few wayward tresses.

For a moment she appeared stricken by his implication; then her features assembled an expressionless mask as she withdrew a tube of coloured gloss from her evening-bag and skilfully smoothed it over her lips.

Without a word she stepped away from him and walked slowly along the terrace to a double set of doors.

For what remained of the evening Georg was never far from her side, and she circulated among the guests, chatting, smiling with such conviction that it was doubtful anyone guessed that inside she was a mess of shattered nerves.

Everyone appeared to be enjoying themselves, but Lexi wondered darkly if it was just a façade. The smiles, the expressed interest all seemed so incredibly false, so artificial. Were any of them true friends, or merely trading as superficial acquaintances? A hollow laugh rose unbidden, then died in her throat. Should anyone present tonight suffer a change in financial status, their social standing would diminish to zero.

'Shall we leave?'

Lexi turned towards Georg and proffered a solemn smile. 'Is it awfully late?'

'Almost two.'

She managed an expression of mock surprise. 'Good heavens. I had no idea.'

A warm, sloping smile tugged at the corners of his mouth. 'Behave, Lexi,' he bade her, and, taking hold of her hand, he led her towards their hosts.

In the car he drove competently, slipping a cassette into the stereo system so that conversation wasn't a necessity, and when he drew to a halt outside her apartment block she made no demur as his hands closed over her shoulders.

She knew she should flee *now*, before she became lost, but it was far too late as his lips brushed hers, settling with unerring ease over their delicate curves, savouring the sensual softness; then she gasped as he caught hold of her lower lip and pulled it gently into his mouth. Her tongue darted forward in a gesture of protective defence, then sprang back in shocked disbelief as he caught its tip between his teeth and gently drew it forward.

She swallowed convulsively, and made a strangled demur in resistance, only to have his mouth open over her own as he took possession in a manner that left her in no doubt as to his ultimate intention.

She reached for his shoulders and used all her strength to push against him, gaining a slight degree of freedom only, she suspected, because he permitted it.

'Please.' The word came out as a tortured whisper.

'You could ask me in.'

'If I did,' she managed shakily, 'you'd read more into the invitation than I intended.'

'And you'd hate yourself in the morning?'

'Something like that.'

She could sense his faint smile a few seconds before his lips brushed hers, then she was free.

'We'll dine out tomorrow night.'

Lexi looked momentarily startled, and was about to refuse when she caught his faintly brooding smile. 'What if I've already made plans?'

'Cancel them,' he instructed cynically.

'I may not want to,' she felt empowered to state, and glimpsed the mockery evident in the depths of his eyes.

'Do it, Lexi. I'll collect you at seven.'

'Do you usually *tell* your female companions what your plans are, and expect them to pander to your every whim?'

His eyes became tinged with musing warmth, and a sloping smile tugged the corners of his mouth. 'For some reason they seem intent on pleasing me.'

She didn't doubt it for a minute. There was an inherent quality about him that was wholly sensual, and something else that made her want to run and hide. Except that she couldn't, and maybe that bothered her more than she was willing to admit.

It was almost as if he was playing a game, she decided with an intuitive flash of speculative knowledge. His manipulative force in the business sector was legendary, and the Press dutifully recorded his every move.

'Why wouldn't they?' Lexi returned sweetly, uncaring of his deep probing glance. 'You're an exceptionally wealthy man, you drive an exotic car, and you're reasonably attractive—if you happen to like a surfeit of brooding Greek magnificence.' She tilted her head to one side as she subjected him to a pensive appraisal. 'I hope I won't damage your ego when I say that it wouldn't really matter if you were fifty, paunchy and bald. The women would still flock to your side.'

One eyebrow slanted in musing cynicism, and she caught a gleam of laughter in the depths of his eyes. 'Perhaps I should return the compliment. There are any number of men waiting to beat a path to your door—if only you would let them.'

Her eyes widened fractionally, then became veiled by the swift downward sweep of her lashes. 'Now you're being facetious.'

'Perhaps we should be grateful that neither of us possess any illusions,' he drawled.

Lexi reached for the doorknob. 'Goodnight.'

She was totally unprepared as he leant forward and covered her mouth with his own.

This time there was no hard possession, more a mixture of evocative control and blatant intention.

She had no defence against the explorative probe of his tongue as it traversed the inner contours of her mouth, and an electrifying awareness tingled through her veins as his touch became so intensely erotic that she had to physically restrain herself from allowing her body its instinctive inclination to lean close in against him and deepen the kiss.

It was madness, and just as she thought she could stand it no longer he lifted his head and slowly pushed her to arm's length.

'Sleep well, Lexi,' he taunted lazily, and in her anxiety she didn't hesitate to escape.

He waited until she was safely through the security doors before restarting the engine, and Lexi walked towards the lift without so much as a backward glance.

How could she *sleep*? He aroused a complexity of emotions, and not one of them was enviable.

Her mouth felt slightly swollen, and she ran the tip of her tongue over the lower curve as she entered her apartment.

Damn Georg Nicolaos, she cursed irreverently. Damn him to hell.

CHAPTER SIX

'You're late,' Lexi greeted Georg the instant she opened the door the following evening.

He pulled back the cuff of his jacket and examined a distinctive gold Rolex. 'Seven minutes. Is it an unforgivable sin?'

It was immaterial that she hadn't been ready until two minutes ago, and she had no intention of informing him of that fact. 'I'm starving,' she declared truthfully, sweeping past him.

'Had a bad day?'

She wanted to hit him, and, enclosed within the confines of the lift, she wondered if there was some dark reason behind the temptation to resort to physical violence whenever she was in his company.

'Shall I start from the beginning?' Even to her own ears she sounded faintly harassed and on edge.

He unlocked the Ferrari and saw her seated inside before going round to slip in behind the wheel and fire the engine. 'Please do.'

'You're amused,' she accused him.

'Intrigued,' he amended as he concentrated on negotiating traffic.

Events of the totally chaotic day rose up to taunt her, and she grimaced in memory. 'The Mercedes had a flat tyre, and I changed it myself. So I was late. That disrupted Jacques's schedule. He swore so...graphically that I thought he was going to cancel the entire session. And nothing went right.

They sent the wrong-sized clothes, and the accessories didn't match. He ordered a few stills in black and white, then stormed out in a temper, leaving us to make the best of it. Monique blasted him with a blistered riposte that would have made a navvy blush.' Her mouth assumed a rueful moue. 'I missed lunch, discovered that the spare tyre I'd substituted this morning had developed a slow leak, and I had to catch a taxi into the city. The modelling academy kept me way beyond the projected time, and do you know how *impossible* it is to get a taxi between five and six?' She suddenly became aware of their whereabouts. 'Where are you taking me?'

'To my apartment.'

'For dinner?'

'Are you unaware that I am an accomplished chef?'

There was nothing she could do to guard against a sharp intake of breath. If she said she'd prefer to go to a restaurant he would imagine she was afraid to be alone with him. And she wasn't. At least, fear didn't motivate the state of her emotions.

'You've been slaving in the kitchen all afternoon?' she countered as he turned beneath an impressive apartment block and sent the Ferrari growling into a reserved bay. 'Don't you have to spend your weekend in an office directing a large slice of the city's finances?'

His smile was faintly cynical. 'I have access to hi-tech equipment in a number of offices, one of which is based in my apartment. Communication in the nineties is becoming increasingly portable. All it takes is the flick of an electronic button.' He switched off the ignition and slid out of the car, waiting until she joined him before walking towards the lifts. 'The restaurant is managed by a team of extremely competent chefs, who kindly permit me to work with them whenever I feel the inclination.' He jabbed the call-button and when the doors slid open he inserted a key to allow private access to the penthouse apartment. 'And slaving is scarcely applicable in preparing a dinner *à deux*,' he concluded as the lift came to a smooth halt.

The penthouse was magnificent, and she said so, complimenting him with genuine sincerity on the tasteful blend of cream, beige and muted shades of brown and Wedgwood blue skilfully used in the décor. Deep-buttoned leather furniture in chocolate brown lent a masculine touch, and contrasting colours were implemented in expensive works of art gracing the walls.

'Sit down,' Georg bade her, crossing to the cocktail bar. 'What can I get you to drink?'

Without doubt there would be wine to accompany their meal, and she had the feeling she needed to be in total control of her senses. 'Something long, cool and non-alcoholic.'

'Playing it safe, Lexi?'

Her eyes caught his, and her chin lifted a fraction in defiance of his drawling tones. 'It's the only way.'

'You sound defensive,' he accorded, slanting her a musing glance. 'Will it help if I assure you that you have nothing to fear?'

Maybe, just maybe she might have believed him if it wasn't for some elusive sixth sense that warned he was skilfully indulging in a contest where he was the mastermind and she merely a pawn. It was crazy, and totally without foundation, but the thought had infiltrated her mind and refused to be dislodged.

'You mean, I'm safe from any so-called "fringe benefits" you might consider your due as a participant in this diabolical scheme?'

His gaze didn't waver, although his eyes darkened measurably, and his voice when he spoke was deliberately mild, yet she detected an edge of steel beneath the velvet-smooth surface. 'As safe as you choose to be.'

If that was assurance it was unsuccessful, and she watched as he put ice in a tall glass, then added lime-juice, a dash of bitters and topped it with soda before handing it to her.

'Good luck.'

Educated in the best private schools, and fashionably 'finished', she was adept at dealing with almost any given situation, commanding an enviable repertoire of stock-in-trade social small talk. Yet with Georg Nicolaos she alternated between raging at him in temper and behaving like a tongue-tied teenager. It was ridiculous, she chided silently.

'Tell me about yourself.'

Lexi looked momentarily startled, and took an appreciative sip from her glass. 'A personal profile from birth until now?' Her lips widened to form a bitter-sweet smile. 'Including a run-down on my disastrous marriage?'

'I consider Paul to be immaterial,' Georg dismissed drily, and she felt a slight shiver feather its way down the length of her spine.

She looked at him carefully, noting the dark business suit, immaculate white linen shirt and sober navy blue silk tie. Character analysis just had to be his forte, for he appeared every inch the wealthy executive, exuding an animalistic sense of power with chilling ease.

'What made you decide to take up modelling?'

Lexi gave a careless shrug. 'It happened by accident. I attended a fashion parade with a friend three years ago. Just after I returned from two years abroad. The mother of another friend owned one of the boutiques supplying the parade with clothes. One of the models failed to show, and I was there— the right height and size. Before I knew it I was out on the catwalk trying to look as if I'd modelled clothes for years.'

'With obvious success,' Georg conceded.

'I enjoyed it,' she admitted. 'Sufficiently so to agree to participating in another fashion parade held a few days later. Jacques was there. He seemed to think I possessed a natural flair. So I began to look at it seriously, enrolling at a modelling academy to learn all the tricks of the trade, and, as they say—the rest is history.'

'It hasn't occurred to you to venture into the field of design?'

'No. It's a cut-throat trade, and you need to be a true artist. I prefer accessories. Matching up shoes, belts, whether to add a scarf and, if so, how it should be worn.' Her eyes had darkened with enthusiasm, and her voice held genuine warmth. 'Jewellery—even the right hairstyle, make-up. The entire composition. I often suggest changes, and Jacques usually goes along with them.'

'All in aid of making women appear beautiful.'

Lexi looked at him, deliberately searching for mockery, yet, if he had intended any, it was carefully hidden.

'A woman's true beauty comes from within,' she revealed slowly. 'It radiates through her skin, shows in her smile, and is reflected in her eyes. If she's not happy with herself, or lacks self-esteem, then it is generally apparent in mannerisms. Body language.' Her gaze became startlingly direct. 'With care and skill a woman can learn to make the best of her natural attributes, no matter what her size or age.'

'Gilding an outer shell, which, with expert marketing, grosses enormous profits for the various merchandisers.'

'Perhaps. But it isn't confined to women. Men like to present the outer trappings of their success in fine clothes.' She ran an experienced eye over his suit. 'Unless I'm mistaken, that's tailored by Ermenegildo Zegna. And your shoes are hand-stitched—either French or Italian imports.'

His smile proved to be a disruptive force, curving his mouth and lightening the harsh lines of his chiselled features. 'Are you implying that I project a required image?'

She responded with a winsome smile. 'Definitely.'

'Which is?'

'An astute entrepreneur,' she ventured quietly. 'Someone who wouldn't suffer fools gladly.'

'What about Georg Nicolaos, the man?'

For some reason she felt as if she'd skated on to dangerously thin ice. 'A contradiction between cruelty and kindness.'

'Ah—*honesty*.' Georg laughed softly, and one glance at those gleaming dark eyes revealed that he wasn't fooled in the slightest.

'Shall we have dinner?'

Lexi needed no second bidding, and she allowed him to lead her to the elegantly appointed dining-room, where within minutes he transferred serving dishes from the kitchen on to the table.

There was soup as a starter, a delicately flavoured leek and potato which tasted like liquid ambrosia, followed by luscious prawns in a delicate sauce served on a bed of rice.

The portions were temptingly small, so that she consumed every morsel, and the main course was an exquisite *coq au vin*.

There was wine—a clear sharp white—and chilled water, and dessert was a superb crème caramel.

'That was—perfect,' Lexi complimented, leaning back in her chair, fully replete.

'A compliment?'

'You can't possibly cook like that every night,' she declared in wistful disbelief, and caught his slow musing smile. 'Do you ever eat alone?' she asked, genuinely curious.

'Not often,' Georg responded indolently. 'I make a practice of dining with Mama once a week, and Samantha and Alex insist I join them on frequent occasions. Anna and Nick, also. Then, of course, the restaurant, and the inevitable social interludes...' He let his voice trail off as he effected an elegant shrug. 'However, there are times when I enjoy a quiet evening at home.'

'Samantha is charming,' Lexi voiced with sincerity.

'She is a very beautiful woman. Genuine, caring. Exceptional.'

Her eyes widened, and she glimpsed the darkness reflected in his own, then he smiled. 'Shall we have coffee?'

'Let's dispense with the dishes first,' she said, getting to her feet and beginning to stack plates together.

'Leave them. My housemaid, Carla, is due tomorrow. She'll attend to them.'

'It won't take long.' She spared him a quick glance. 'Unless you're particularly protective about a woman invading your kitchen?'

Shrugging off his jacket, he tossed it carelessly over a nearby chair, and she watched as he removed cufflinks and folded back the sleeves of his shirt.

'In that case, we'll do them together.'

The kitchen was a delight, spacious and boasting every modern convenience imaginable. Apart from a collection of saucepans drying in a dish-rack atop the draining-board, there wasn't a thing out of place.

'I'm impressed.'

'With the kitchen?'

His faint mockery did strange things to her equilibrium, and she concentrated on rinsing the crockery and cutlery while he stacked the dishwasher.

'What made you decide to be a chef?'

'My parents emigrated from Greece when Alex, Anna and I were very young. Papa owned three restaurants in Athens, and it was a natural progression for him to pursue the business here.' He filled the percolator with water, extracted a filter and spooned in freshly ground coffee beans. 'We all helped, waiting tables, the dishes, cleaning. Before school, after school, during semester breaks. Like all parents, they wanted great things for each of their children, and I followed Alex into university and studied for a business degree. Papa was taken ill not long after I graduated, and for a few years I worked in an office by day and managed the restaurant at night. Now we keep it for Mama's sake. It represents so many memories for us all.'

'She must be very proud of you.'

'We are a very close family.'

The strength of her own familial ties was such that she'd consented to an impossible charade with a man who was the antithesis of harmless.

'All done.' Lexi dried her hands, then watched as Georg set cups on to their saucers, then extracted sugar, liqueur and cream. His hands were large, and his forearms firmly muscled and liberally sprinkled with dark hair. Their actions displayed an economy of movement, and there was strength apparent as well as a degree of sensitivity.

'Come into the lounge.'

Said the spider to the fly, she echoed silently, wondering what quirk of cynical humour had promoted that thought to mind. 'I must leave soon,' she murmured out loud, and incurred his dark slanting glance.

'Must?'

'I need my beauty sleep,' she quipped lightly as she followed him and settled comfortably into a single armchair.

'We also need to plan the next week,' Georg indicated as he took an opposite chair. 'It was the reason I brought you here, so that we could discuss it rationally rather than risk argument in a public restaurant.'

'I don't argue,' Lexi retaliated, only to give a rueful smile as she caught his raised eyebrow. 'Well, not usually.'

'I'm the exception?'

She looked at him carefully. 'Just because I recognise the necessity for this ... deception——' she paused deliberately '—doesn't mean I have to like it.'

The dark eyes sharpened, and for some inexplicable reason she had difficulty holding their concentrated gaze.

'You find me—dislikeable?'

She suddenly felt as if she'd stepped from the safe shallows into water way over her head. 'No,' she said honestly.

'Yet you're afraid.'

It was a statement she didn't deny. She had genuinely enjoyed his company tonight, even if she had been slightly on edge. And, if she was fair, she could only accord that fault as entirely her own.

'I don't feel entirely comfortable with you,' she admitted, and saw his eyelids droop slightly, successfully veiling his expression.

'Could that not be because we have yet to forge a friendship?'

Could a woman ever be mere *friend* to someone like Georg Nicolaos? Somehow she doubted it.

'You mentioned collaborating on our social calendar.' Lexi broached the subject in an attempt to steer the conversation into safer channels.

'There are the inevitable invitations issued at this time of year,' he drawled, 'few of which I usually accept. However, there is a party to be held at the home of a friend which I think we should attend. Samantha and Alex have requested that we join them at a society ball, the proceeds from which are donated to make Christmas a more joyful occasion for a number of terminally ill children. It is considered to be *the* social event of the season.'

'Good heavens,' Lexi said faintly. 'I'm due to fly to the Gold Coast on Thursday morning for a photographic shoot organised by the Mirage Resort. It will be followed early in the New Year by another at the sister resort in Port Douglas.'

Georg's eyes narrowed faintly. 'How long will you be away?'

She gave a slight shrug. 'Overnight, on each occasion.'

'Apart from that do you have any social obligations?'

She looked at him, noting the apparent indolence, and wasn't fooled in the slightest. 'Jonathan, David and I usually attend a few pre-Christmas functions together.' A faint sigh whispered from her lips. 'I think I prefer an evening of solitude with a good book, or tuned in to a VCR.'

'I can think of an infinitely more pleasurable way in which to spend the night hours,' Georg drawled, and saw the faint blush of pink that crept into her cheeks.

'I'm sure you can,' Lexi managed equably. With unhurried movements she stood to her feet. 'Would you mind if I phoned for a taxi?'

His eyes trapped her own for far too long, and she had to glance away from that disturbing gaze. 'You haven't finished your coffee.'

He was imperturbable, so maddeningly calm, and totally impervious to the agitation welling deep inside her. Lexi suddenly felt as if she were treading on eggshells.

'Please.' She attempted to keep her voice light and devoid of a degree of mounting tension. 'I'd really like to leave.'

'As soon as I finish my coffee I'll take you home.'

Reaching forward, she picked up the cup and saucer, spacing her movements so they appeared calm and unhurried as she sipped the remaining brew, then she carried the cup out to the kitchen and carefully rinsed it.

When she turned he was there, and her pulse began an erratic beat as he moved close to place his cup and saucer in the sink. It simply wasn't fair that she was overly sensitive to his potent brand of sexuality.

'Ready?'

She gave an indicative nod, and without a further word he turned and preceded her from the apartment.

In the car she sat in silence, consumed by an acute sense of vulnerability. A number of conversational gambits rose to mind, but she ventured none of them, and she sat trapped in silence for a few interminable seconds as he brought the Ferrari to a halt outside her apartment block.

'Thanks for dinner.' Good manners insisted that she acknowledge his hospitality.

'So—thank me.'

She looked at him carefully, and wondered why she should suddenly feel threatened. All she had to do was reach forward and place her lips to his cheek.

Except that he turned his head and her lips touched his mouth, and before she could retreat he lifted his hands to capture her head, and it was he who took command, *he* who turned what began as a casual salutation into an evocative embrace that made her aware of a magical, elusive alchemy.

A treacherous weakness invaded her limbs as he wrought havoc with a ravaging exploration that brought a thousand tiny nerve-endings leaping into pulsating life, arousing feelings too complex to distinguish any one as she clung to him unashamedly.

It was almost as if every pore of her skin became suffused with sweet aching pleasure beneath his mercilessly erotic plunder of her senses, and when at last he slowly released her she could only look at him in complete bewilderment.

Without a word she reached for the door-handle and slid out from the passenger seat.

The door snapped shut with a refined click, and she crossed to the main entrance without a backward glance, using her security card to gain access; it was only when she was safely indoors that she heard the muted roar of the Ferrari's engine as it purred down one half of the semi-circular driveway.

It was a relief to enter her apartment, and she secured the lock before crossing to the windows to close the curtains against the night sky.

She felt incredibly restless, and far too emotionally uptight to sleep. Perhaps a long, leisurely soak in the spa-bath might ease some of her tension, and without further thought she wandered into the bathroom and filled the capacious tub.

Half an hour later she emerged to towel herself dry, then, attired in a short cotton nightshirt, she slipped into bed to lie staring into the darkness for what seemed an age, before exhaustion finally claimed her in a deep, troubled sleep from which she woke late, dark-eyed and drained.

During the following few days Lexi deliberately maintained a low profile. She consulted with Jacques over the forthcoming shoot at the Gold Coast's tourist resort, met Jonathan for lunch, completed some Christmas shopping, and spent an hour stretched out on a lounger beside the pool each afternoon, perfecting a tan. For two consecutive evenings she conjured up a suitable excuse to avoid seeing Georg, and on the third night she answered the doorbell to find him standing in the hallway.

'Have you eaten yet?' he drawled, and Lexi looked at him with exasperation as he moved into the lounge.

'I planned on spending a quiet evening at home.'

One eyebrow slanted in quizzical disbelief. 'You've already done that two evenings in a row.'

She heaved a faint sigh. 'Is that an indication we should go out and play?'

'What if I say...you get to choose the venue?'

'You're taking an awful risk,' Lexi declared. 'I may decide on a rock concert.'

'Out of sheer perversity?'

'Yes, I think so.' Humour lent her hazel-gold eyes an impish sparkle and she tilted her head to one side. 'You'll have to change. Where we're going, anything else but jeans, T-shirt and joggers will be a fashion mis-statement.'

'You have tickets?'

A wide smile curved her mouth. 'Indeed. Jacques did an outrageously successful shoot a few years ago for one of the leading agencies in town. Ever since, they've presented him with half a dozen tickets to each top promotion.'

'I hardly dare ask which bands are featured,' he drawled, almost wincing as she named two; then she added insult to injury by following them with three artists known for their explosive style on stage. 'This is revenge, I gather?'

'I sat through *Madame Butterfly*,' she reminded him, and saw his eyes darken with cynical humour.

'I doubt there is any comparison.'

'It starts at eight.'

'You're determined?'

The thought of having him suffer through hours of impossibly loud rock music was too great a temptation to miss! 'Yes.'

'Then get changed, and we'll go back to my apartment.'

'After which, when you've changed into casual gear, we'll go straight on and grab a hamburger or eat something there.' She saw his look of disbelief and managed to appear completely guileless. 'Be a devil for once. I'm sure your digestive system will survive.'

'More pertinent: will my eardrums?'

'Oh, I think so,' Lexi declared solemnly. 'I've been to a number of rock concerts, and my hearing is still intact.' She gestured towards the drinks cabinet. 'Fix yourself something while I go change.'

Ten minutes later she emerged clad in faded denims, a white T-shirt, white jogging shoes, and a denim jacket slung casually across her shoulders. Make-up was minimal and she'd twisted her hair into an elaborate pleat at her nape.

'I suspect I'm in for a culture shock,' Georg drawled as he followed her out of the apartment, and she spared him a laughing glance.

The Ferrari traversed the short distance between Darling Point and Double Bay in record time, and Lexi watched the news on television while Georg effected a swift change of clothes.

'Hmm,' she accorded musingly as he re-entered the lounge a short while later. 'You look almost—human.'

He certainly looked different, having discarded the image of impeccably attired businessman for something infinitely more casual. Hip- and thigh-hugging jeans worn with a pale cotton shirt beneath a contrasting designer jacket was perfectly suitable attire in which to attend a rock concert. Yet somehow it failed to disguise the essence of the man and his innate ability to project an aura of power.

'It would take only minutes to grill steak and prepare a salad.'

'Hamburgers,' Lexi negated firmly, moving towards the lobby.

'Junk food.'

'Surveys report there's not as much junk in *junk* food as we're led to believe. It can actually be quite high in nutritional value.' She wrinkled her nose at him. 'Relax, Georg. You may just enjoy yourself.'

That Lexi did was without doubt. The music was loud, but the sound-effects were without distortion, emitted at their sophisticated best and an audible attestation to superb technology. She clapped and sang with the rest of the audience, oblivious for the most part to the man who sat at her side.

'Isn't he great?' Lexi enthused as one of Australia's better-known vocalists took the stage for a popular encore—a song that had won him an Entertainer of the Year award the previous year. He was married, a devoted husband and father, and affectionately held his doting public in the palm of his hand. 'He doesn't just *sing*—he puts everything into it and becomes a part of the music itself.' She turned towards Georg and was disconcerted to see that his attention was centred on her, not the band or the vocalist on stage. For a moment her breath locked in her throat as she became trapped by the expression in those dark eyes, then she swallowed and said fiercely, 'The proceeds of this concert go to charity.'

'You don't need to justify anything,' Georg drawled. 'And you're right. I am enjoying myself—watching you.'

She felt incredibly vulnerable, and everything else faded as she glimpsed something she dared not define before she managed to tear her gaze away.

The musicians caught her attention, but for the remainder of the evening she was supremely conscious of his presence.

It was late when the concert wound down, and the exits became jammed with a river of people attempting to vacate the venue. It was even worse trying to leave the car park.

Consequently it was after midnight before the Ferrari was able to move freely in traffic, and Lexi leaned well back in her seat and closed her eyes as she mentally reviewed the concert and its artists.

'Do you want to go somewhere for supper?'

She opened her eyes and turned to look at him. 'Are you hungry?'

'Peckish.'

'We're not exactly dressed for any of your usual haunts,' she ventured.

'I know of a place. Trust me.'

When the car slid to a halt she checked their whereabouts and shot him a cheeky grin. 'I don't believe this.'

'Come on. Out.' He slid from behind the wheel and went round to open her door. 'A fitting end to the evening, wouldn't you say?'

The café was intimately small and spotlessly clean, and the smell of food was tantalising. They sat opposite each other in a booth, and ordered steakburgers, fries and salad. Afterwards they washed it down with surprisingly good coffee, then Georg paid the bill and drove towards Darling Point.

It had been a wonderful evening, and she told him as much as he drew to a halt outside her apartment block.

'I agree.'

Something in the tone of his voice arrested her attention, and she turned towards him in seemingly slow motion as his hands caught hold of her shoulders.

'Georg—don't. Please,' she whispered as he impelled her forward, and the butterflies in her stomach began an erratic tattoo, making her frighteningly aware of the electric tension between them.

Lexi felt herself begin to tremble as he lowered his head and touched his lips briefly against her temple.

Any further protest became lost as his mouth slid down to cover hers in a kiss that was tantalising, tender, yet with a hint of controlled passion, and to her utter chagrin it left her feeling vaguely bereft and wanting more.

'I really must go,' she said a trifle shakily.

'Don't forget we're attending the charity ball tomorrow night,' Georg reminded her as she made to step out from the car. 'We're meeting Samantha and Alex there at eight. I'll pick you up at seven-thirty.'

She murmured agreement, then activated her security card to pass through the main doors, and when she turned back all she could see was the twin red tail-lights as the Ferrari swept down the street.

CHAPTER SEVEN

LEXI dressed with care, and her mirrored reflection gave visual satisfaction that her choice of gown was a success.

In midnight-blue silk, it accentuated her slim curves by hugging them shamelessly from breast to knee before flaring out in a generous fold that fell to ankle-length. Matching shoes and evening-bag completed the outfit, and for jewellery she'd opted to wear a glorious sapphire pendant encircled in diamonds and matching ear-studs.

Her hair was worn swept back from her face and caught together at one side so that a thick mass of curls cascaded down on to her left breast. Make-up had been skilfully applied to highlight her eyes, and a deep dusky rose coloured the generous curve of her mouth.

Perfume—Jean-Louis Scherrer—completed the required image, and at the sound of the doorbell she moved through the lounge to answer its summons.

'Beautiful,' Georg accorded softly, after conducting a slow appreciative appraisal that brought a defiant sparkle to her eyes.

'Wearing clothes is an acquired flair,' Lexi qualified with a faint defensive lift of her chin as she met his warm gaze.

'You do it extremely well.'

Perhaps she'd overdone it, she decided wryly. Except that tonight of all nights, given such an auspicious occasion, she felt the need to excel. The charity ball would be patronised by the cream of Sydney's society, and Lexi Harrison's affair with Georg Nicolaos was hot gossip. She would be examined in detail from the tip of her shoes to the top of her head, discussed and dissected, her behaviour observed and criticised. From the moment she stepped out of Georg's car she would need to *shine*.

'Would you like a drink?' she queried. 'Or shall we leave?'

'Oh, leave, I think,' Georg intimated with husky humour. 'Otherwise I shall probably be tempted to dissuade you from moving one step out of this apartment.'

The only way she could cope with him in this frame of mood was outright flippancy. 'And waste all the time and effort I've expended in adopting this glamorous image? Not on your life.'

'Shame,' he drawled. 'Now I shall have to exercise the utmost control during the entire evening.'

She proffered a wide sweet smile. 'I have no doubt you'll manage.'

He stood to one side, allowing her to precede him into the lobby.

The venue was a plush hotel in the inner city, and, although she had attended many such functions in the past, tonight it was impossible to dispel a feeling of nervousness.

Georg Nicolaos had a lot to answer for, she decided darkly as they moved into the foyer, where their tickets were scrutinised and marked off an impressive list before they were ushered into the elaborately decorated function-room.

Drinks and canapés were served by a bevy of hovering waiters, and Lexi drifted at Georg's side as they slowly mixed and mingled with a variety of acquaintances.

'Lexi; Georg.' Alex, with Samantha at his side looking incredibly lovely in black velvet. Lexi greeted them both warmly, accepted Samantha's compliment and promptly returned it. 'Shall we take our seats at the table?' Alex enquired. 'It looks as if most of the guests are intent on becoming seated.'

The food was superb, and Lexi forked a few mouthfuls from each course, declined wine in favour of mineral water, and opted for fresh fruit salad instead of the cheeseboard. There were the usual salutary speeches lauding the charity chairperson, the secretary, and a brief résumé of the charity's successful endeavours and anticipatory projections. Then it was clearly party-time as a band took up its position and began to play.

'Would you excuse me while I freshen up?' said Lexi.

'I'll come with you,' Samantha indicated, rising to her feet, and together they began threading their way across the room.

The powder-room was crowded, and it took considerable time before Samantha was able to occupy a spare cubicle. Lexi gave her place to an expectant mother who obviously needed to use the facilities more urgently than she did.

'Don't wait,' Lexi bade Samantha with a helpless smile. 'I'll rejoin you as soon as I can.'

It was at least five minutes before she emerged, and she paused as someone called her name, then stood politely as a woman she barely knew insisted on offering her congratulations.

An acquaintance of Jonathan's restricted her passage, enquiring after his health, and she turned to retrace her steps to the table.

Afterwards she couldn't recall quite what made her conduct a sweeping appraisal of the function-room and its guests. She certainly wasn't conscious of doing it deliberately. There had to be at least thirty people present whom she knew reasonably well, and more than fifty who were social acquaintances.

Even as her eyes skimmed the crowd, it never occurred to her that she might number her ex-husband among the invited guests.

Lexi felt the blood drain from her face at the sight of Paul standing on the far side of the room. Even from this distance she could see the wicked, faintly malevolent gleam in his eyes, the cynical twist of his mouth.

She saw him murmur to his companion, then he began threading his way through the gathered groups of guests.

'Well, hello,' Paul greeted softly, and she cringed beneath his deliberate raking appraisal. 'It's been ages, my sweet. I see you're inhabiting the social scene again,' he intoned hatefully. 'The gossip around town is that you and Georg Nicolaos are an item. Are you?'

Careful, she cautioned silently. The last thing she wanted was a scene. Perhaps if she was polite he'd be satisfied and leave her alone.

Lexi took her time in answering, letting her lashes sweep up as she met his stare with unblinking solemnity. 'Yes.'

His lips curved to form a vicious sickle. 'Why, Lexi, darling, whatever are you thinking of? Georg eats little girls for breakfast.'

'I'm no longer a little girl, Paul,' she said steadily. 'You personally saw to it that I grew up.'

'Do you imagine for one minute it will be any different with Georg Nicolaos? He's a hard corporate executive, too attuned to business interests to be much concerned with *you*, except when it suits him, of course.'

'As you were, Paul?'

'My, my,' he accorded with slow deliberation. 'Tell me, sweetie,' he began, pausing as he set his weapons ready for the figurative kill, 'are you still an inhibited, frigid little bitch in bed? Or hasn't Georg been able to persuade you into his yet?' He reached out a hand to push back a tendril of hair behind her ear, and laughed softly as she reared back from his touch as if from flame.

'You would be advised not to cause trouble, Ellis,' a too-familiar voice intimated with icy disdain, and Lexi felt faint.

'I have an invitation to this soirée,' Paul said mockingly, his eyes moving slowly from Georg to Lexi.

'Obviously,' Georg conceded with studied ruthlessness. 'Otherwise you would not have been admitted.' He paused, before adding with killing softness, 'However, if I hear of your bothering Lexi again I can promise that you will live to regret it.'

Lexi shivered at the degree of ice evident in Georg's tone, and she glimpsed the malevolent gleam in Paul's eye as he ventured cynically, 'Physical violence, my dear chap?'

'Nothing so uncivilised.'

Paul's gaze swept down to the ring on Lexi's finger, then he lifted his head to slant her a mocking glance. 'Congratulations, darling. Daddy will be pleased.'

It was evident that Paul had deliberately sought this very scene, and Lexi was supremely conscious of the curious looks cast in their direction, the avid, all-too-seeing eyes alight with speculative conjecture. Inside she was shattering into a thousand pieces, but she was darned if she'd give Paul the pleasure of glimpsing any visible signs of her distress.

'Yes,' she agreed quietly, 'he is.'

'Better luck this time, sweetie.'

'We'll excuse you,' Georg said silkily. 'There can be no doubt this conversation has reached its conclusion.'

'I wouldn't dream of continuing it,' Paul declared with ill-concealed mockery, then he turned and strolled with apparent nonchalance to rejoin his friends.

Pride was a damnable thing, and she lifted her head, tilting her chin in an unconscious gesture of defence. Georg's eyes seemed to tear down the barriers she had erected, and after a few interminably long minutes she lowered her gaze to a point somewhere above his left shoulder.

Without a word he reached out and caught hold of her hand, and she shifted her attention, meeting his unfathomable expression with a clear, direct gaze, hiding the pain buried deep inside. She even managed a slight smile, although she was unaware that it appeared to be tinged with sadness. 'The only regret I have where Paul is concerned is that I was foolish enough to be taken in by him in the first place.'

'You were young and susceptible, were you not?'

Lexi gave an imperceptible shrug. 'Nothing alters the fact that I made a terrible misjudgement of character, which was only compounded by my unwillingness to heed my father or David.'

'You paid for your mistake.'

It wasn't a query, merely a statement of fact, and her lashes swept down to shutter the sudden flaring of pain.

'Not all men are callous, insensitive brutes,' Georg offered quietly.

'Possibly not.' She paused, her eyes wide and startlingly direct. 'But I've never been sufficiently inclined to set out on a wild bedroom romp in an attempt to disprove Paul's accusations of my frigidity!'

'Ludicrous,' Georg drawled, and her eyes flashed with sudden animosity. 'That you could possibly be frigid,' he elaborated.

'And you're an expert on the sexual exploits of men and women?'

His faint smile held amused cynicism. 'I can guarantee that my experience is infinitely more vast than yours.'

'I wouldn't dream of doubting it!'

He lifted her hand to his lips and idly brushed her fingertips in a gesture that was blatantly evocative, and she felt so impossibly angry it was all she could do not to snatch her hand from his grasp.

'Stop opposing me,' he berated quietly.

'How can I *not* oppose you? At first it appeared I was agreeing to a simple collusion,' she said wretchedly. 'Now I'm wearing an engagement ring, and you've told Jonathan and the gossip columnists that we're getting married within weeks!'

'Would it be so disastrous if we did?'

Her eyes widened with incredulous disbelief. 'You can't be serious?'

'Very serious.'

'But—*why*?'

'Why not?' Georg countered smoothly. 'I look at Alex and Samantha and I know that I want what they have. A caring relationship; children.'

'That's no basis for marriage,' she responded, utterly shocked by his reasoning.

'Isn't it better to have a marriage based on friendship and mutual trust than chase an illusion?' His eyes were dark and fathomless. 'I have amassed considerable assets. Do you think for one moment that women solicit my attention for reasons other than with an eye to a generous expense account, travel, and the gift of limitless jewellery?' His query was wholly cynical, and she looked at him carefully.

'You would be content with such a relationship?'

'Yes.'

Her expression registered an entire gamut of emotions, and she struggled to contain them. Could she marry him? *Dared* she? Once she had chased a fairy-tale and fallen flat on her face. Maybe this time she should use her head instead of her heart.

He smiled, and everything else seemed to fade as he leant forward and brushed his lips against her forehead. 'I'll get you a drink,' he said solemnly. 'And then we'll mingle.'

Lexi accepted a glass of champagne, then walked at his side as they mixed with the guests, pausing to converse with one group and another before eventually rejoining Samantha and Alex.

'Shall we leave them to it?' Samantha queried with a cheeky grin as the two brothers became engaged in deep conversation, and Lexi agreed, watching as Samantha briefly touched Alex's shoulder.

Georg caught the unobtrusive gesture, and his eyes pierced Lexi's for a second before he returned his attention to the man at his side.

Together Samantha and Lexi threaded their way towards a table where two waitresses were dispensing coffee.

'Oh, this is heaven,' Samantha breathed as she sipped the aromatic brew. 'It has been a successful night. All the tickets were sold out last week.'

'Another notable charity,' Lexi accorded. 'Georg seems to be an active patron of several.'

'Georg is a very special man,' Samantha offered with deep sincerity.

'He complimented you in much the same manner.'

A dimpled smile turned Samantha's features into something quite beautiful. 'We are—*simpatico*. There was a time when Alex was impossibly jealous. Completely without foundation, I might add.'

'Of course.'

Samantha laughed. 'You sound so sure.'

'One has only to look at you and Alex together to know no one else in the world exists for either of you.'

'Yet it wasn't always like that.'

Lexi didn't know what to say, and sagely maintained her silence.

'I found myself married to Alex without any choice,' Samantha revealed quietly. 'I was very young, and at first I rebelled. Rather badly, I'm afraid. The first few months were——' she paused, effecting a faint grimace in memory '——difficult.'

'You weren't in love with him?'

'Not at first, no.'

'I find that very hard to believe.'

'Now I cannot imagine my life without him.'

Lexi looked at her carefully. 'What are you trying to tell me?'

'That Georg is the one man, aside from Alex, whom I would trust with my life,' Samantha said simply.

'You think I'm not sure of Georg?'

'I think,' Samantha corrected, 'you're unsure of yourself.'

'Oh, my,' Lexi declared with a defenceless little shrug. 'Next you'll say that love can come after the marriage, and I should leap in where any self-respecting angel would fear to tread!' Her eyes kindled with rueful cynicism, and Samantha laughed.

'Are we permitted to share the joke?' a deep voice drawled from behind, and Lexi turned to see Alex and Georg had rejoined them.

'Most definitely not.'

'Ah—woman-talk, I presume,' Alex declared, shooting his wife a dark probing glance that held latent warmth.

'We were talking about men,' Samantha reported gravely.

Her husband seemed interested, rivetingly so. 'Indeed?'

Georg began to laugh softly, and caught hold of Lexi's hand. 'I think we'll leave you two alone.' He tugged gently, and drew her towards the dance-floor.

'I'm not sure that I want to dance,' Lexi protested, yet somehow she was in his arms, and the music was slow, the lights low, and it was all too easy to forget everything except the moment.

His hold was less than conventional, and after a few minutes she gave in to temptation and let her head rest against the curve of his shoulder. If she closed her eyes she could almost imagine this was real, and somewhere deep inside was born the longing for it to be more than just a pretence.

There were as many reasons why she should marry him as there were reasons for her to refuse. She thought of Samantha and Alex, and their daughter Leanne; of a home, with Georg in the role of husband, lover, father.

'You're very quiet.'

Lexi lifted her head and gave him a rueful smile. 'I was just about to suggest we leave. It must be after midnight, and I have to catch an early-morning flight to the Gold Coast.'

'We'll find Samantha and Alex, and bid them goodnight,' Georg declared, relinquishing his hold.

Ten minutes later they were in the car, and Lexi sat in silence, listening to the slight swish of tyres traversing a road wet with a sudden summer shower of rain. The air smelt fresh and clean, and the sky was a clear indigo blue, almost black, and even as she looked there was a sprinkling of stars to herald the promise of a clear new day.

Georg brought the Ferrari to a halt outside the entrance to her apartment block and switched off the engine.

'I'll ring you as soon as I get back,' Lexi indicated as she released the seatbelt.

'Ring me when you arrive,' he drawled, releasing his own and shifting slightly to face her.

He seemed to loom large, a vaguely threatening force, and she mentally chided herself for possessing too vivid an imagination.

'I have to pack,' she said quickly.

'And you merely want to escape.'

She looked at him carefully, seeing his rough-chiselled features, the stark strength apparent. 'It's quite late.'

'Then kiss me goodnight, and run upstairs to bed.'

She felt her eyes widen, and wondered at the degree of indolent sensuality apparent in his voice.

'Why so hesitant, Lexi?' he drawled. 'Have I suddenly grown horns?'

She shook her head. 'Of course not,' she negated slowly.

'Yet you find it difficult, hmm?'

You can't begin to know *how* difficult, she longed to respond, then she gave herself a mental shake.

This was crazy. Tentatively she reached up to brush her lips against his cheek, and found he'd moved his head so that instead she encountered his mouth.

For a moment she froze, then she pressed her mouth lightly against his in a fleeting kiss.

'That isn't exactly what I had in mind.'

His faint mockery brought a flood of colour to her cheeks, and she opened her mouth to fling a stinging retort at him only to have it possessed by his in a kiss that rocked the very foundation of her being. 'Possessed' was the only word adequate to define it, and some devious alchemy had to be responsible for the traitorous way she began to respond. Her breathing became rapid and uneven, and she was aware of the pulse thudding at the base of her throat. Every inch of skin tingled alive, heightening her senses and making her feel achingly aware of him until she wanted more than a mere melding of mouths.

The restriction of clothes—his, *hers*—seemed an impossible barrier, and her fingers shook as they hovered close to his shirt buttons, then fell away in distracted dismay as she realised how close she was to wanting him totally.

With a murmur of distress Lexi tore her mouth away. Her eyes were impossibly wide and hauntingly luminous and her cheeks tinged with pink as she encountered his dark glittering gaze.

'If you don't want me to come upstairs and invade your bed I suggest you get out of the car before I discard my noble instincts,' Georg taunted with husky amusement.

Lexi needed no second bidding, and she heard his soft chuckle an instant before she closed the door behind her and ran lightly towards the entrance.

CHAPTER EIGHT

IT HAD been quite a day, one way and another, Lexi mused thoughtfully as she entered the luxurious apartment. The sun at its zenith had been hot—at least three degrees higher than Sydney temperatures, and she needed a cool shower and an icy drink.

The Gold Coast was one of her favourite places, its relaxed lifestyle and long hours of sunshine providing a magnet for the many tourists who flocked to the famed coastal strip in search of golden sands and sapphire-blue sea with spume-crested waves rolling in from the Pacific Ocean. Many of the shopping complexes favoured seven-day trading, and it was all too easy to lose track of time exploring exotic boutiques in any one of several malls.

With a faintly weary gesture Lexi reached a hand to the long thick length of her hair and lifted it away from her nape. The apartment's air-conditioning cooled the heat from her skin, which, despite liberal use of sunblock during the long hours spent in the sun, showed visible signs of exposure.

The photographic shoot had been successful, and a brief session in the morning should wrap it up, then she would be able to catch the next available flight home.

A strange anticipatory thrill coursed through her veins at the mere thought, and she was forced to admit reluctantly that Georg was the main cause.

His image was never far from her mind, and she had only to close her eyes to instantly recall his strong features, the depth of his eyes and the degree of lazy warmth in his smile.

Was it all merely a pretence in their scheme of make-believe? she wondered as she stripped off her clothes and stepped into the shower cubicle. Selecting shampoo, she began working it into the thick length of her hair.

There were times when she rather wistfully longed for their supposed romance to be real, yet that was akin to chasing an impossible dream. The reality was more...comfortable, she decided. If 'comfortable' was a description one could apply to Georg Nicolaos! He possessed the ability to set her emotions into pure turmoil with the least amount of effort.

Lexi sluiced shampoo from her hair, then repeated the process and worked in conditioning lotion.

It was impossible to dispel the fact that he probably regarded her as an attractive addition to his life; if they married she would assume the role of hostess and companion who conveniently fulfilled his sexual needs.

Could such an arrangement work? Would she be able to live with him, accept his physical love-making without becoming too emotionally involved?

Damn. The soft curse was lost beneath the sound of the shower as she deliberately cast such evocative thoughts aside and concentrated on completing her ablutions.

Several minutes later she donned a silk robe before plugging in the hairdrier to style her hair.

A time-consuming task, which she had almost completed when the doorbell rang, and a puzzled frown momentarily creased her forehead as she moved through the lounge. She hadn't ordered room-service, and she certainly wasn't expecting anyone.

The tall dark frame filling the aperture was incredibly familiar.

Her surprise was evident, and several differing emotions chased fleetingly across her expressive features. 'Georg! What are you doing here?'

'Aren't you going to ask me in?'

His slight smile did strange things to her equilibrium, and she stood aside at once. 'Of course.' She pushed a hand through her hair, and gave a faint grimace. Tumbled tresses, no make-up, and attired in only a robe. He couldn't have caught her at more of a disadvantage if he'd tried. 'I haven't long emerged from the shower.'

His eyes were strangely watchful as he reached forward and trailed his fingers down the smoothness of her cheek. 'You look about sixteen,' he said quietly, and she wrinkled her nose at him in silent admonition, feeling suddenly gauche at the degree of drawled amusement in his voice, and a little nervous.

'This is a surprise,' she declared lightly. 'Can I get you a drink?'

'I'll fix myself something while you get changed.'

Something in his tone ensured that he was the total focus of her attention, and her eyes flew to his with a mixture of concern and outright fear.

Unbidden, her hand rose towards him, then fluttered down to her side. 'It's Jonathan, isn't it?'

'He collapsed this afternoon,' Georg revealed gently. 'At this very moment he's in surgery. I chartered a private jet from Sydney, and a limousine is waiting outside. All you have to do is slip into some clothes.'

'David——'

'Is waiting for us at the hospital.' He leaned forward and brushed his lips against her temple. 'Jonathan will be fine,' he reassured. 'He has the best team of vascular surgeons in the country, and they're confident of success.'

There wasn't a thing she was capable of saying, and she turned away from him blindly, her movements completely automatic as she walked swiftly into the bedroom.

Retrieving a bag from the wardrobe, she hurriedly tore clothes from their hangers, then she slipped into clean underwear and donned eau de Nil cotton trousers and matching top, slid a brush through her hair and slipped her feet into casual shoes. She could attend to her make-up in the limousine, she decided, gathering up toiletries and her make-up bag.

'I've arranged your check-out,' Georg informed as she emerged into the lounge. 'Is there anyone here you should contact before we leave?'

'The cameraman. He's staying in a unit at the resort.'

'Give me his name, and we'll arrange for a message to reach him.'

Two hours later they arrived at Sydney airport, and it was after eight when they reached the hospital to find a weary, but mildly exuberant David waiting to greet them.

Lexi flew into his embrace at once, and was soundly hugged before being gently pushed to arm's length.

'Jonathan's OK,' David reassured her before she could voice the query. 'Surgery was successful, and he's in intensive care.'

Intensive care sounded vaguely frightening, and she stood still, hugging herself in a defensive gesture as she looked askance from one to the other in silence.

'Standard procedure,' Georg assured her quietly. 'They'll keep him there for a few days until he stabilises, I imagine.'

A shiver shook her slim frame. Life was so tenuous, so incredibly fragile. The thought of losing Jonathan was more than she could bear. 'Can I see him?'

'I'm sure the medical staff would advise against it,' Georg said gently. 'He'll be heavily sedated, and hooked up to various machines.'

She turned towards her brother. 'David?'

'Georg is right, sweetheart. There's nothing we can do.' He reached out and gave her shoulder a gentle squeeze. 'Let Georg take you home. The hospital has my number, and if there's even the slightest change I'll call you at once.'

In the car she sat in silence, and it was only when the Ferrari drew to a halt that she withdrew from reflective thought sufficiently to recognise her surroundings.

Indoors, she made for the lift, conscious that Georg walked at her side, and she made no demur when he took her keys and unlocked the apartment.

'Thank you,' she said with genuine gratitude. 'For ensuring that I reached Sydney as quickly as possible.'

'I'll fix a snack,' Georg indicated. 'You ate nothing on the plane.'

'I don't feel hungry.'

'Something light,' he insisted as he shrugged off his jacket, and, placing it over a nearby chair, he rolled up each sleeve-cuff and walked into the kitchen. 'An omelette?'

Lexi slowly followed him, watching as he deftly set the pan to heat, whisked eggs in a bowl, then sliced up bacon, cheese and tomato.

Within minutes she found herself seated at the table, forking delectable pieces of food into her mouth. It was delicious, and she said so, shooting him a slight smile as he made the coffee.

'You're more than just a handsome face,' she accorded lightly.

'Ah—a compliment,' he drawled as he poured the aromatic brew into two cups. 'Usually you are swift to upbraid me for some imagined misdemeanour.'

She spared him a direct look, and was disconcerted by his unwavering gaze. 'We—strike sparks off each other,' she ventured in explanation, and heard his husky laugh.

'Have you ever paused to consider *why*?'

'I resent you,' Lexi responded swiftly. 'For attempting to rule my life—*me*.' Replacing her cutlery on her plate, she pushed it towards the centre of the table. 'In a minute we'll be arguing again.'

'Something at which you seem to excel.'

She looked at him carefully, seeing the strength apparent and an indomitable measure of self-will. 'I don't feel inclined to be at cross purposes with you tonight.'

'In that case, let's take our coffee into the lounge and watch television together.'

She shrugged slightly. 'Why not?'

For the next hour they sat in separate chairs, watching the second half of a film, and when it finished Georg got to his feet.

A strange sense of desolation assailed her at the thought that he was about to leave, and she rose from the chair, then stood hesitantly as he took the few steps necessary to bring him within touching distance.

He had only to reach out, and she waited, almost afraid to breathe, alternately craving solace and unwilling to accept its price.

For a long time she just looked at him, watching with detached fascination as he lifted a hand and brushed his fingers across the delicate planes of her cheek, then lowered his head.

His kiss held an infinite degree of *tendresse*, and she felt the ache of tears. Never had she felt quite so alone or so incredibly forlorn, and she badly needed to hold on to his sheer physical presence.

He held her gaze, and she stood mesmerised, unable to look away from those deep dark depths as if her life depended on it. He tilted her face, framing it between his hands, and his gaze was steady. 'Do you want me to stay?'

'I—don't think I could bear to be alone,' she whispered, feeling shaky and ill-equipped to deal with him.

Her lips parted, trembling a little as he idly traced their lower curve. Unbidden, her eyes filled with tears, and he swore softly as they spilled over and ran slowly down each cheek. Lexi shook her head slightly, and rubbed the back of her hands across each cheek. 'It's just reaction.'

He pressed a forefinger against her mouth, and his eyes darkened as he felt her lips tremble beneath his touch.

'I'll heat some milk and brandy,' he said gently.

She was powerless to prevent the lump that rose in her throat, and she merely nodded in silent acquiescence, watching as he left the room.

Dear heaven, she was weary. If she could just close her eyes for a few minutes...

When Georg re-entered the lounge she was asleep, curled up on the sofa, looking as guileless as a young child.

A slow smile tugged at the edges of his mouth, and he carefully eased her slight body into his arms and carried her through to the bedroom.

She stirred faintly, but didn't wake as he slipped off her outer clothes and placed her between soft percale sheets.

He stood looking down at her for a very long time, then he moved quietly into the main bathroom and showered before switching off the lights with the exception of one in the hallway.

Lexi slept deeply, caught up in the spell of differing dreams, some more vivid and vaguely disturbing than others, and she was barely aware of a source of enveloping strength as she hovered increasingly closer to wakefulness.

There was something different apparent, but she was unable to pinpoint exactly what, until the powerful heartbeat beneath her cheek gradually penetrated her subconscious, and she froze, becoming aware with shocking clarity that she was not only in bed, but held lightly imprisoned against a male body. What was more, one of her arms curved across the hard musculature of his ribcage, while one of *his* closed possessively over her hip.

'You're awake.'

If she lay perfectly still maybe her immobility would persuade him he was mistaken.

'Don't pretend,' Georg drawled. 'Your heartbeat has just gone into overdrive.'

As if to prove his point he trailed a hand to the rapidly beating pulse at the base of her throat.

With infinite slowness her lashes swept slowly upwards. Her lips felt impossibly dry, and she drew in the lower curve in an attempt to moisten it. Inside she was as nervous as a kitten, and her eyes clung to his as he tilted her chin.

'What are you doing here?' Her voice quivered slightly, and her eyes widened as she viewed him with unblinking solemnity.

The reflection from the lighted hallway provided subdued illumination, and she glimpsed his faint smile.

'Your apartment, specifically, or your bed?'

Her throat ached, and the words came out in a husky undertone. 'Don't—tease.'

His fingers trailed a gentle exploratory path across the delicate hollows at the base of her throat.

His touch was familiar, and so very sure, that the blood drained from her face. He hadn't—surely they hadn't——? No, it wasn't possible. She would have woken, would have known——

'You think I would attempt to steal from you in sleep what you would not willingly give when you were in total possession of your senses?'

Dear lord, was she so transparent? Heat flooded her cheeks, and her lashes swept down to form a protective veil.

His warm breath fanned her temples. 'Lexi?'

She heard the softly voiced command, and was held immobile by the wealth of seduction apparent. She looked at him, and she wanted to cry, but no tears would come.

Capturing her head between his hands, he leant forward and covered her lips with his own, softly and with such tenderness that it made her catch her breath. There seemed no urgency to deepen the kiss as he gently traced the outline of her lips, savouring their sweet fullness until her mouth parted of its own volition.

Without conscious thought her hands slid to his shoulders, then crept up to encircle his neck, and his mouth hardened in possession as he sought a devastation that left her weak-willed and malleable.

It seemed an age before he relinquished her mouth, and he trailed his lips down the sensitive cord at her neck to explore the hollows at the base of her throat, then edged lower to the curve of her breast.

The top she wore was easily dispensed with, as was the silk and lace that comprised her bra, and she gasped as he captured one tender burgeoning peak between his teeth and rendered such exquisite pleasure that it was all she could do not to cry out. Her fingers raked through his hair, silently begging him to desist as her whole body began to pulsate with molten fire, and she became mindless, lost in a wealth of sensuality so intense that there was no room for anything else but the need to subside into the swirling vortex of emotion.

There could be no turning back, and she told herself that nothing else mattered, only *now*, as he gently removed every last vestige of her clothing.

His hands and his mouth became evocative instruments as he sought to awaken a tumultuous response, his lips grazing down over her ribcage on a destructive path towards the central core of her femininity.

Her shocked protest went unheeded, as with deliberate eroticism he taught her to enjoy an experience so fraught with sensual ecstasy that she cried out, alternately pleading for more and begging him to desist, until, just as she thought she could stand it no longer, his mouth began a slow upward trail, tantalising, teasing, tasting.

Slowly, with care, he gained entry with one sure thrust, then he deliberately sought a response she was afraid to give.

Her pleasure began as a spiralling sensation that swelled into an intense throbbing ache as she became completely and utterly absorbed in his deep rhythmic possession.

Mindlessly exultant, she scaled the heights of ecstasy and knew she never wanted to descend from this elusive sensory plateau where sheer sensation ruled.

Her faint whimper of distress was very real as he began to withdraw, and she held him close, unwilling to have it end.

His lips moved to her shoulder, caressing the delicate curves and hollows, before wandering with tactile sensuality to tease the edge of her mouth; then he lifted a hand to her chin and forced her to meet his gaze.

There wasn't a single word she was capable of uttering, and her eyes felt like huge liquid pools mirroring the degree of deep slumberous passion she'd experienced beneath his touch.

Gently he lifted her hand to his lips, and there was nothing she could do to prevent the slight quivering of her mouth as she glimpsed the warmth reflected in the depths of his eyes.

It was impossible for him to be unaware of her unbridled response to his lovemaking, and a faint tide of pink coloured her cheeks as she glimpsed his slight smile.

This, *this* was so different from Paul's selfish insensitivity, Lexi decided wondrously, feeling bewitched and bemused by the awakening of her own sensuality. She had read once that good lovemaking was nature's ultimate aphrodisiac, and it was true, for she felt tremendously and utterly *complete*.

Her eyes widened slightly as Georg slid out of the bed, and anything she might have said was lost beneath the brief pressure of his mouth; then he straightened and walked towards the *en suite* bathroom. She let her lashes drift, down, unwilling to move so much as an inch.

Minutes later her eyes flew wide open and she made a slight sound in protest as she was lifted out of the bed and carried into the bathroom.

Without any effort he stepped into the round spa-bath and lowered her to sit in front of him. Deliciously warm water lapped her shoulders, and it was pure reflex action that sent her hands to her hair, lifting, twisting its length into a knot atop her head.

She wasn't capable of uttering a single word as he collected soap and began slowly sponging her skin. The action was gently erotic, and she felt a traitorous warmth unfurl deep within and steal treacherously through her veins.

His lips grazed across her exposed nape and settled in the soft curve of her neck, then travelled to the tip of her shoulder and trailed back again. One hand cupped the slight fullness of her breast, while the other traced an evocative pattern across her ribcage, then ventured lower to settle with unerring ease on the nub of her femininity.

Nothing seemed to matter except the resurging desire spiralling through her body, emcompassing and all-consuming, and she gave a startled gasp as he lifted her round to face him.

He kissed her, gently at first, then with tantalising evocativeness, choosing not to allow her to deepen the kiss until she murmured a protest and captured his head with her hands.

His eyes gleamed with lazy passion as she moved forward, and he allowed her licence to initiate a foray that somehow became his to control, then he gently broke the kiss, smiling faintly at her disappointment.

For a moment she was unsure of his intention, and her eyes widened in disbelief as he carefully positioned her to accept his male length, and he watched several fleeting emotions chase expressively over her features as his manhood swelled inside her.

Then his hands slid to her breasts, shaping the soft curves before rendering exquisite torture to their engorged peaks.

Just as she thought she could stand it no longer, he slid one hand to her nape while the other tangled in the mass of her hair as he pulled her head down to his, and this time his kiss was an erotic possession that gave no quarter until she became a mindless supplicant in his arms.

It was a long time before they emerged to towel each other dry, then they walked arm in arm to the bedroom and slid into bed to continue the long slow exploration until sleep claimed them at the edge of a new day's dawn.

CHAPTER NINE

LEXI felt a featherlight touch tracing a delicate pattern along her collarbone, and she opened her eyes slowly, unwilling to come fully awake in case what she'd experienced last night had been little more than a figment of her vivid imagination.

'Wake up, sleepyhead.'

Dreams didn't have voices that sounded like a deep, teasing faintly accented drawl belonging to a certain Greek—at least, none of the dreams she'd ever experienced.

Slowly she let her eyelashes sweep upwards, and her eyes widened slightly as they met the lazy warmth reflecting in his.

'Good morning,' Georg greeted her gently.

She couldn't think of one coherent word to offer, and his mouth assumed a sensual curve that tripped her pulse-beat and sent it racing at a rapid rate.

Thanks, she wanted to say, for the most beautiful night of my life. Except that her throat was dry, and she doubted that any sound would emerge.

'Orange juice? Coffee?' he slanted musingly, shifting slightly to prop his head with one hand.

She wanted both, except she was loath to move, and he laughed softly as he reached out to push several tumbled tresses back behind her ear.

'Time to rise and shine,' he mocked huskily. 'I have a meeting to attend at nine-thirty, and I imagine you want to ring the hospital.'

Jonathan. Dear lord, how could she possibly have forgotten? Her eyes mirrored her anguish, and he leant forward to brush his lips across her mouth.

'David hasn't rung, so Jonathan's condition will be stable.' He pushed the sheet back and bent to bestow a lingering kiss on her breast. 'Let's take a shower, then we'll share breakfast.'

There was nothing she could do to prevent the faint tinge of pink that flew to her cheeks at the promise of shared intimacy, and the colour deepened as Georg slid out from the bed, unconcerned by his nakedness, and walked round to scoop her into his arms.

'Put me down,' Lexi protested half-heartedly, and he merely laughed as he carried her through to the bathroom.

Reaching into the shower-cubicle, he turned on the taps then let her slide to her feet in front of him.

'You're shy.'

As a statement of fact it was without equal, and she gave a slight ineffectual gesture of assent.

'Don't begin erecting barriers, Lexi.'

She felt utterly defenceless, and she swallowed convulsively as her mouth began to tremble. 'I'm not—used to this,' she said shakily.

His eyes flared, and she saw the pupils darken and change as he caught her close. Then his mouth opened over hers in a kiss that possessed every nuance of erotic mastery, skilfully absorbing her until nothing else mattered except *now*.

She had no idea how long they remained locked together, and when he slowly broke the kiss she could only stand in total bemusement as he reached for a shower-cap, pushed the mass of her curling hair beneath it and gently pulled her into the cubicle.

Half an hour later they were both dressed and seated opposite each other at the breakfast table.

Jonathan, the hospital reported, was stable and had spent a comfortable night. Visitors were limited to five minutes and restricted to immediate family.

Almost as soon as she had replaced the receiver David rang through with the same news and suggested she meet him for lunch.

'I'll see you tonight about seven,' Georg bade her as he drained the last of his coffee.

'Where?' Lexi queried idly as she walked with him towards the door, and he smiled down at her.

'My apartment . . . yours—does it matter?'

Her eyes lifted to meet his, and she looked unsure, not really wanting him to leave, yet knowing that he must.

'We'll discuss it tonight. Take care,' he said quietly as he opened the door.

Then he was gone, and Lexi closed the door behind him before wandering back into the kitchen.

The day held a dream-like quality as she attended to routine chores, made a few calls, rang David and confirmed arrangements for lunch, then drove to the hospital.

Jonathan was still heavily sedated, and, although he opened his eyes during her brief visit, she doubted her presence registered.

David was already seated when she entered the small restaurant, and he rose to his feet with a warm smile creasing his attractive features.

'I had trouble parking,' she explained with an expressive shrug as she brushed her lips to his cheek. He shook his head as he told her, 'I've only been waiting a few minutes. Will you have something to drink?'

'Mineral water.'

They each ordered from the menu, and Lexi opted for a garden salad followed with fresh fruit.

'How are you getting on with Georg?'

'Reasonably well,' Lexi acknowledged cautiously.

'Jonathan is absolutely delighted you've both opted for marriage,' David ventured, shooting her a deep probing look that didn't fool her in the slightest. 'You must know you have my blessing.'

She took a leisurely sip from her glass, then replaced it carefully down on the table. 'I'm sure you and Jonathan are immensely relieved.'

David appeared to choose his words carefully. 'We've both known the Nicolaos family for many years.'

'How is the business deal progressing with the Japanese consortium?'

'Extremely well. Alex and Georg have managed to elicit a signed preliminary agreement, which I have perused and sanctioned. As soon as Jonathan is well enough the documents will be presented for his signature.' He lifted his shoulders in an expressive gesture. 'Aside from time-consuming technicalities, it is virtually a *fait accompli*.'

She picked at her salad and forked a few morsels into her mouth before venturing, 'And Paul? Presumably you've managed to come to an amicable arrangement with him?'

'We're in a state of negotiation.'

'He's pressing for a larger settlement, and you're stalling,' Lexi deduced with a wry grimace.

'For a few more days, until the deal is due for a Press release,' David agreed.

'After which he will have no room for further negotiation.'

'Precisely.'

It was impossible to refrain from cynicism. 'And all loose ends will be successfully tied.'

'A propitious start to a productive new year.'

'It's Christmas the day after tomorrow,' Lexi murmured, and her expressive eyes dulled slightly as she became lost in reflective thought, remembering previous years at home with numerous gifts piled beneath an enormous decorated tree and Sophie dishing up a veritable feast of festive fare. 'It won't be the same with Jonathan in hospital.'

'I've already spoken with Sophie, and we'll have lunch together at the house, then spend time with Jonathan. Georg, I'm sure, will insist you share the evening with his family.'

She was gripped with a sudden need to confide her own doubts and insecurities. 'David...' she paused, unsure whether her choice of words would sound inane '...I'd rather this marriage was planned for months down the track, instead of the mere weeks Georg is insistent upon.'

Her brother assumed a look of professionally bland inscrutability. 'It's perfectly understandable you should experience doubts, given the circumstances. Why not discuss them with Georg?'

'Because he's equally clever as you, if not more so,' she acknowledged quietly, and he offered her a slightly whimsical smile.

'Shall we order coffee? I'm due in court at two.'

'David——'

'Marry him, Lexi,' he advised gently. 'I'm confident you'll never have cause to regret it.'

How could something appear so simple and logical, yet be fraught with innumerable complexities? Lexi pondered as she drove to the hospital and called in on Jonathan.

This time he was awake, but extremely drowsy, and she was cheered by his faint smile and the reassurance by nursing staff as to his progress.

What remained of the afternoon she spent shopping, and she returned to her apartment laden with various coloured carrier-bags and packages which she spilled on to the bed in the spare bedroom.

It was hot—so hot, in fact, that Lexi decided to change into a bikini and swim several leisurely lengths of the swimming-pool in an effort to cool off and relax, before returning to her apartment to shower and wash her hair.

Would Georg want to dine in, or go out? Out seemed infinitely safer, for she needed time to think about their shared intimacy and all that it implied before accepting a state of domesticity and shared domicile.

She was ready a few minutes before seven, dressed in an elegant cream strapless silk gown with matching accessories. A silk wrap completed the outfit, and she added a slim gold choker, bracelet and ear-studs. A last-minute check in the mirror lent reassurance that she'd made the right decision in adopting an intricate upswept hairstyle, and her make-up was understated, with skilled application of shadow and liner to emphasis her eyes.

For some reason she felt consumed by nervous tension, and when the doorbell pealed she took a deep breath before crossing the lounge.

Georg looked the epitome of the sophisticated executive, and she let her eyes sweep over the impeccable tailoring of his suit before lifting her gaze to meet his.

Then she immediately wished she hadn't, for she wasn't quite prepared for the lazy warmth evident in those dark eyes or the sensual curve of his mouth. It brought a vivid reminder of all that they'd shared through the night, and her senses leapt at the thought of what lay ahead at the evening's end.

'I wasn't sure what you had in mind,' Lexi offered helplessly, and a husky chuckle left his throat.

'Oh, just an enjoyable meal in your company,' he drawled, adding softly, 'for now.'

Her eyes widened at his unspoken implication, and she was powerless to prevent the feeling of acute vulnerability. 'Would you like a drink?'

His smile deepened, and her stomach seemed to execute a series of somersaults as he caught hold of her hand. 'If you're ready we'll leave.'

The restaurant Georg had chosen was one of the city's élite establishments, and he ordered expensive champagne, then asked her choice of food before selecting what proved to be an epicurean delight.

They conversed, discussing the highlights of each other's day among other things, and afterwards Lexi had no clear recollection of a single topic.

All she was aware of was Georg. His expressive features, the wide-spaced dark eyes, the broad well-defined bone-structure, and his mouth, which seemed to compel an almost hypnotic fascination.

It was after ten when they left, and Lexi was grateful when he slotted a tape into the cassette-player, for it meant she didn't have to search for something adequate by way of conversation.

On reaching her apartment block, he simply parked the car and together they took the lift to her designated floor. She was incapable of making any demur when he retrieved her keys, unlocked the door, then ushered her inside.

All evening she had been conscious of his indolent regard, the degree of latent passion evident, and now she felt like a finely tuned violin waiting for the maestro's touch. It was crazy to be so acutely aware of another human body and the effect it could have on her senses.

'You look so incredibly fragile I am almost afraid to touch you,' Georg mused as he lifted a hand and trailed his fingers down her cheek. He traced the curve of her mouth with a gentle forefinger, then lowered his head to bestow a fleeting kiss on her mouth.

Her lips parted involuntarily, trembling as she caught his indrawn breath, and she felt a sense of loss as he drew back and stood regarding her with disruptive sensuality.

'Will you object if I unpin your hair?'

She shook her head in silent acquiescence, and when the curls lay in a thick mass below her shoulders he slid his fingers through their length.

'I've wanted to do this all evening.'

And I've waited all day, she assured silently, and felt vaguely shocked at the truth of her thoughts.

Then he kissed her, gently at first, and afterwards she had little recollection of who was in command as passion flared and demanded assuagement.

With a husky exultant laugh Georg swept her into his arms and carried her through to the bedroom, where he took infinite care to remove every last vestige of her clothing before beginning on his own.

Lexi behaved like a shameless wanton beneath his touch as he sought to strike an unhitherto heard chord, and she cried out as the deep rhythm of his possession took her to the heights of ecstasy and beyond.

Long after he had fallen asleep at her side she lay awake, too caught up with introspection to cull an easy somnolence.

Even now it seemed a fantasy, some wild imaginative dream that had no part of reality. Potent, dangerous, and—in its aftermath—destructive.

Just as she'd thought the pain and degradation Paul had inflicted was unacceptable, this— passionate *possession* Georg evoked was everything she'd been led to believe, and more.

Had *he* felt like that? Was he able to command such a mindless response from every woman he took to bed? Or was it merely sexual chemistry at its zenith? She'd been so caught up with her own reactions that she hadn't given a thought to his.

A shudder shook her slender frame in the realisation that she'd taken everything he'd chosen to give, and given nothing in return. It had been *her* pleasure, her climactic orgasm that had been all-important, the desperate need to have him continue arousing those spiralling sensations until she felt almost *driven* by a wholly consuming desire.

In the night he stirred and reached for her, settling her into the curve of his body, and she woke late to find an empty space beside her and a scrawled note on the adjoining pillow, which read, 'Dinner tonight my apartment—I'll cook. Georg.'

Lexi showered, then, dressed in casual clothes, she drove to the supermarket, battling against weary mothers with young children and middle-aged matrons in an effort to traverse the numerous aisles and fill her trolley with necessary groceries. She visited Jonathan in hospital, then she returned home to tidy up before driving back to the hospital mid-afteroon.

It was almost six-thirty when she buzzed Georg's apartment from the lobby, and within minutes the lift descended to transport her to the uppermost floor.

She had elected to dress casually, choosing a straight black skirt and white knit top, and her hair was caught up at her nape with a fashionable black bow.

'Mmm, smells heavenly,' Lexi greeted him as soon as Georg opened the door, and she almost melted at the warmth reflected in his eyes.

'Tonight you will sample a selection of traditional Greek cuisine.'

'And afterwards can we watch the carol-singing on television?' she ventured, wriggling her nose at him as he slanted her a quizzical glance. 'It's Christmas Eve.'

He, too, was in casual attire: dressed in designer jeans and a cotton-knit shirt, he projected a raw virility that was arresting.

For a starter he served vine-wrapped parcels of minced lamb accompanied by a delicate sauce, which he followed with moussaka. Dessert was baklava, and afterwards they dispensed with the dishes before taking their coffee through to the lounge, where they watched a number of artists, accompanied by a choir, sing a variety of carols, recorded live from a large city park.

'I must go,' Lexi intimated when the programme came to a close.

'Why must you?' Georg drawled.

'Tomorrow is Christmas Day,' she said helplessly as he reached forward and undid the bow fastening her hair. 'I'm visiting Jonathan in the morning, and meeting David at the house at midday. After lunch we'll both go to the hospital, and——'

'Stay with me,' he interceded. 'And in the morning we will visit Jonathan together.'

She looked at him carefully, then opened her mouth to speak, only to have him press her lips closed.

'Indulge me. I cannot think of a nicer Christmas present than to wake and find you in my bed.'

A long time afterwards she wondered why she hadn't protested, but by then it was far too late to rationalise her decision.

Christmas Day was filled with love and laughter, the joy of gifts and giving, *family*. Hers, his. And Jonathan was progressing with such speed that it seemed there was little cause to doubt his ability to recover fully from surgery.

The days leading up to New Year passed all too quickly. Lexi spent each morning and afternoon visiting Jonathan, and the nights were spent with Georg, at his apartment or her own. Sometimes they ate out, dining with Samantha and Alex, or with Mrs Nicolaos, and when they stayed home they took it in turns to prepare the evening meal.

'I'll cook tonight,' Lexi declared as she followed him to the door of his apartment a few days before she was due to fly north for the photographic shoot at the Port Douglas Mirage Resort. She had something special in mind, and teased lightly as he moved towards the lift, 'Will you mind if I use your kitchen?'

'Carla is due to arrive about nine,' he warned as he pressed the call-button.

His housekeeper was Spanish, matronly, and came in two days a week to clean, stock up the pantry and refrigerator from Georg's list, and take care of the laundry. She was a delight, voluble, and possessed of a wicked sense of humour.

Lexi retreated into the kitchen and poured herself a second cup of coffee, then planned a menu and checked ingredients before making out a list of what she needed.

At ten she visited Jonathan, then went on to complete her shopping, and most of the afternoon was spent preparing food.

Carla left at five, and Lexi hurriedly changed into white evening culottes and a patterned top before returning to the kitchen to anxiously oversee the various dishes alternately simmering atop the elements and the oven. Then she was able to centre her attention on setting an elegant table in the dining-room.

When Georg arrived shortly after six everything was ready, and she felt inordinately pleased with the result.

'Hmm, is this is a sample of what I can look forward to in the future?' he drawled as he caught her close, and she returned his kiss with such fervour it left her slightly breathless.

'I felt like surprising you,' she said simply, and her bones seemed to melt at the warmth reflected in his eyes.

'Mental telepathy, perhaps?' Georg slanted as he moved across to the cabinet to pour them both a drink. 'I have decided to surprise you by having an agent line up a few properties for us to inspect tomorrow.'

Her expressive features portrayed a gamut of emotions. 'You intend buying a house?'

'Yes, Lexi. *Ours.*'

She took the slim crystal flute from his hand and sipped the contents. 'I assumed if we married that we'd live here.'

His gaze probed hers. '*When*, not if. And we shall live here until such time as the redecorating and refurbishing of the house is completed.'

The breath caught in her throat, and for a moment she was lost for words. 'I barely become accustomed to one concept when you confront me with another,' she managed shakily.

He reached out and tilted her chin. 'I thought I had managed to dispense with all your doubts.'

She gave a light shrugging gesture. 'Most of them.'

Gently he bent his head down to hers and trailed his lips over her cheek. 'Could it be that you need reassurance?'

'The kind of reassurance you have in mind will mean we get to miss dinner,' she reproved him with a helpless smile, and he laughed softly.

'Tonight you have gone to too much trouble for that, hmm?' His kiss was hard and brief, then he stepped back and caught hold of her hand. 'Let us eat.'

If not exactly of cordon bleu standard, the meal was a complete success, and Lexi basked in the glow of Georg's praise as he sampled one course after another before sitting back, replete, with a glass of superb port.

Together they dispensed with the dishes, and after a leisurely coffee Georg simply swung her into his arms and carried her through to the bedroom.

CHAPTER TEN

THERE was no doubt which house held the most appeal. Lexi fell in love with its Federation-style architecture and multi-coloured leaded windows, the many rooms with wide glass doors opening on to a magnificent terrace, and the panoramic view of the harbour. Possessed of an air of tranquillity, it seemed far removed from the city's hustle and bustle, and with its gardens pruned and replanted it would soon be restored to its former glory.

'This is it?' Georg queried, smiling at her enthusiasm.

'It has so much potential,' she breathed. 'What do *you* think?'

'I'll contact the agent this afternoon.'

'I have a few things to do,' Lexi declared as Georg headed the Ferrari towards Double Bay. 'Shopping.' She really could not leave selecting a suitable gown for the wedding any longer, and she knew of just the boutique where she might find exactly what she had in mind. 'And I'll call into the hospital to see Jonathan, then head back to my apartment.'

'Don't forget we're dining out tonight,' he reminded her. 'I'll collect you at six.'

It was after four when Lexi entered her apartment, and she moved through to the kitchen to retrieve a cool drink from the refrigerator. As much as she adored shopping, to do so in the heat

161

of sub-tropical summer proved an enervating experience.

The insistent burr of the telephone sounded loud in the stillness of the apartment, and she quickly crossed the room and picked up the receiver.

'Lexi?'

The sound of Paul's voice was totally unexpected, and her fingers tightened until the knuckles showed white.

'You must know I have nothing whatsoever to say to you,' she reiterated hardily.

'You don't need to, darling. Just listen is all I ask.'

'Hurry up and get it over with, Paul. I haven't much spare time.'

'Jonathan's precious deal has gone through. Although I guess you know that. And I've been paid off,' he drawled. 'Not as handsomely as I'd like, but adequately enough.'

'Is that it?'

'Don't hang up, Lexi. This conversation is entirely for your benefit.'

She gave a heavy sigh. 'I find that almost impossible to believe.'

'Ah, but you see, darling,' Paul informed her hatefully, 'what you fail to comprehend is that the ultimate joke in this entire débâcle is on you. *Yes*, my sweet——' he paused to give his words sufficient emphasis '——a masterly scheme, conveniently compounded by *my* coincidental involvement, for, after your initial disastrous foray into matrimony with me, it became essential such an error was not repeated. Your dear father and brother, in cohorts with Georg, conspired to utilise

Jonathan's forthcoming surgery as a reason to arrange an eminently suitable marriage for you—with none other than Georg Nicolaos.' His laugh was totally without humour. 'And you, in your innocence, played right into their hands.'

She felt sickened, almost to the point of being physically ill. It took considerable effort to keep her voice calm, but she managed it—just.

'I don't have to listen to any of this.' She had surpassed anger, and was fast approaching a numbed state of limbo.

'Check it out with David,' Paul exhorted cynically. 'I doubt he'll deny it.' Lexi didn't bother to comment, and he continued in a hateful voice, 'Will you think me facetious if I wish you happiness in your second marriage? Such a pity its basis is no more to do with *love* than your first,' he accorded, and there was a slight click as he hung up.

Lexi stood where she was for several long seconds, then she depressed the call-button and punched out a succession of digits.

'David Harrison,' she requested as soon as the receptionist answered. 'Lexi Harrison speaking.'

'Mr Harrison is engaged with a client. Can I get him to call you?'

'It's urgent,' Lexi insisted, and seconds later David came on the line. 'Paul rang to tell me he'd been paid off,' she began without preamble. 'He insists Jonathan deliberately conspired with you and Georg to trap me into marriage. Is it true?'

There was an imperceptible silence, and her stomach gave a sickening lurch.

'Your happiness has always been Jonathan's prime concern,' David responded cautiously.

'Don't play the courtroom tactician with me, David,' she said tightly. 'At least have the decency to confirm or deny it.'

'It's clearly evident you and Georg are happy together.'

'Damn you!' she cursed. 'That doesn't excuse anything!'

'I'll call Georg——'

'Don't interfere,' she warned fiercely. 'If you do I'll never speak to you again!'

She replaced the receiver and almost immediately the telephone burred an insistent summons. For all of ten seconds she determined not to answer, and only the thought that it might be Jonathan motivated her to pick up the receiver.

'Lexi?' Georg's deep faintly accented voice sounded so close he could have been in the same room. 'I'll be delayed by about half an hour.'

Oh, heavens, they were supposed to be dining out! She closed her eyes, then slowly reopened them. 'I was just about to ring you,' she declared, inventing with no scruple whatsoever. 'I can't make it tonight. Jacques needs me. One of the models reported in sick.'

She closed her eyes momentarily against the slight throbbing that began in the region of her right temple.

'Where is the assignment? I'll meet you there.'

An inner voice screamed out in silent rejection. She couldn't face seeing him tonight. If she did she'd never contain the anger that was seething deep inside. 'No, Georg.' Time enough tomorrow to face a confrontation. By then she might have gathered sufficient courage to be able to adopt a cool rationale. 'I have to go. I'm running late.' She replaced the receiver before he had a chance to comment. Crossing into the bedroom, she stripped off her outer clothes, then selected designer jeans and a loose cotton top at random from her wardrobe. Dressed, she caught her hair into a loose knot, picked up her bag, and made her way out of the apartment.

Quite where she was heading she wasn't sure. Anywhere would do, as long as she had some time alone in which to think. Somewhere where no one could contact her.

In the car she slotted a compact disc into the music system, then sent the Mercedes up to street level. Taking a left turn, she simply drove, uncaring of her direction or destination.

Sheer driving skill and instinct kept her within the speed limit and observant of the road rules. Either that or divine guidance, she decided wryly as she finally brought the car to a halt on the side of the road.

She had no idea where she was, for how long or how far she'd travelled, and she rested her forehead on the steering-wheel in a gesture of infinite weariness.

Perhaps there was a motel somewhere nearby where she could book in for the night. It was either that or face a long drive back to her apartment.

A strange light-headedness assailed her, and she wound down the window to let in some fresh air. Now that she thought about it, the last time she'd eaten was at midday, and then it had only been a light salad.

A glance at her watch revealed that it was nine o'clock. She'd been driving for more than three hours.

It was hardly likely that anything would be open at this time of night, although she vaguely remembered passing a petrol station a short while ago. Maybe they ran a fast-food outlet where she could pick up hot coffee and a filled roll.

Without further thought she switched on the ignition and fired the engine, swinging the car in a semi-circle on to the northbound highway.

Half an hour later, suitably revived by two cups of strong coffee and a surprisingly wholesome meal, she made the decision to drive home.

It was almost one o'clock when she took the lift up to her apartment. As the doors slid open she stifled a yawn, weary almost beyond belief.

At first she didn't see the tall figure leaning against the wall outside her apartment door. It wasn't until a slight movement caught her attention that his presence registered, and she faltered mid-step, then froze as Georg's muscular frame unfolded.

Shock, resentment, *anger*—all those emotions seemed to register at once, and her tiredness vanished.

'What are you doing here?'

One eyebrow slanted in silent query. 'Whatever happened to "hello"?' His gaze was dark and infinitely formidable beneath its steady appraisal. 'I contacted Jacques, only to be told that, if there was a fashion parade on in the city tonight, he certainly wasn't running it.' His eyes seemed to mesmerise hers. 'If you didn't want to dine out you had only to say so.'

Lexi didn't blink. 'You would have asked questions and demanded answers.'

His silence accelerated her nervous tension to a point where she was sure he must see the pulse thudding at the base of her throat. 'Do you consider it so strange that I feel I have a right to know if something bothers you?'

His drawled query seemed like the last straw! Her anger snapped, and she could feel it erupt inside her like a volcano. *'Right?'* she exploded. 'You have no rights where I'm concerned!'

His gaze narrowed, and a muscle tensed along the edge of his jaw. 'The hallway is hardly the place for a slanging match. Where are your keys?'

Ignoring her protest, he took her bag and searched inside it until he discovered her keyring, then he calmly put an arm around her waist and hoisted her over his shoulder.

'Put me down, you fiend!' She tried to kick him and one of her shoes fell to the carpeted floor. 'Let me go, *damn you*!'

There was nothing she could do to stop him unlocking the front door, and, once inside, he closed it with an almost silent click before allowing her to slide down to her feet.

His eyes held hers, dark and incredibly watchful. 'Now, suppose you explain?' he demanded in a voice that was dangerously soft.

'Explain?' she vented, furious almost beyond belief. 'You thought you were very clever, didn't you? Together with Jonathan and David, you played both ends against the middle and manu-

factured a conspiracy in which you were not only
a perpetrator, but a willing participant.' Her eyes
gleamed with a fine rage. 'You conniving, uncaring, diabolical *bastard*! Who do you think you
are, attempting to play God?' She took a step
forward and began railing him with her fists, hitting
him anywhere she could connect—his chest, his
arms, his shoulders . . . beating him with an anger
that brought tears streaming down her cheeks until
hard hands caught hold of her own, stilling their
actions with galling ease.

'That's enough.'

'I hate you!' she stormed vehemently. '*Hate* you,
do you understand?'

His hands tightened their grasp on her wrists, and
she struggled powerlessly against him as he drew
her close. Effortlessly he caught both her hands
together, then slid his hand through the length of
her hair, exerting sufficient pressure until there was
no other option but for her to meet his gaze.

Lexi was aware of every muscle in the taut length
of his body, and she wanted to scream and rage
against him.

Broken dreams, a cynical inner voice taunted; the
destruction of the hope that Georg could possibly
feel about her the way she felt about him, that such
a tenuous, precious emotion as *love* might be
shared.

Yet pride forbade acceptance of any logic, and
she pulled away from him, straining against hands
that held her firmly at arm's length.

'Let me go,' she demanded, attempting to wrest
free from his grasp and failing miserably.

'So that you can run away again?'

'I didn't run,' she disclaimed heatedly, and glimpsed the wry twist of his mouth.

'No?'

'Will you please leave?' she countered with un-accustomed hauteur. 'I'm tired, I have a headache, and I want to go to bed.' Her eyes resembled fiery shards of sheer topaz, a brilliance that refused to be daunted beneath his probing gaze. She felt mentally drained, and completely enervated. The headache was no fabrication, and she raised a shaky hand to her left temple in an attempt to ease the pain.

'I would have thought you impervious to any element of gossip,' Georg drawled with soft inflexibility.

Her eyes didn't waver from his for a second. 'Paul was terribly convincing.' She saw the dark flaring in the depths of his eyes, the faint bunching of muscle at the edge of his jaw. 'Yes, *Paul*. But then, you know, don't you? I have no doubt David called you, in spite of anything I said to the contrary.' She lifted a hand in an involuntary gesture as he would have spoken. 'Don't. Please don't compound the situation with any mean-ingless qualification.' She even managed a faint smile. 'It's amazing, really. Beneath the anger, the sheer *rage* that my life, my future, should be treated with such clinical detachment and utter high-handedness, I can still see the logic of it all from Jonathan's point of view. The youngest child, his adored little girl, couldn't be allowed to drift through life alone. A man had to be found: the *right* man. Someone above reproach, of considerable financial standing, and preferably of a similar calibre to Jonathan himself.' Her features assumed a deliberately winsome expression. 'Even fate took a hand in providing the perfect opportunity to have me collaborate. Bypass surgery is sufficiently serious to warrant respect and a willingness to ease the patient's mind. I can even understand Jonathan's need to tie it all up beforehand, so that *he* could undergo surgery safe in the knowledge there would be someone to care for me should things go wrong. What I fail to comprehend,' she continued slowly, 'is *your* involvement. You don't need my share of my father's money. You're so self-sufficient, you certainly don't need *me*. And I refuse to believe you'd consent to marry merely to honour the close friendship of a business partner.' She drew in a slight breath, not caring just how brutal her analytical dissection became. 'There is, of course, the possibility you had reached an age where you were inclined to make the clinical decision to take a wife and sire a son to follow in your footsteps. In that respect I guess I qualify. I'm from the right side of the track, educated, personable. We're even physically——'

'Compatible?'

Remembering exactly to what precise degree they were sexually in tune almost proved to be her undoing, and a faint tinge of pink rose to define her cheekbones. 'Yes.'

'Is that how you see me?'

Her chin lifted fractionally as she accorded without guile, 'I have to give you full marks for sensual expertise.'

His eyes seared hers, almost as if he could see through to her soul. 'You think that's all it was?' he demanded in a voice that sounded like steel razing silk asunder.

'Good sex,' she conceded matter-of-factly. Inside she was slowly dying. 'I doubt it comes any better.'

'The mechanical coupling of two consenting adults who indulge in an act of physical lust? Not making love, where each partner takes infinite care to caress and arouse until they ache with an awareness so acute it transcends mere pleasure? And even then the pleasure is extended until the fire becomes unbearable, like a mindless passion demanding the release that only they can give—to each other?'

Lexi wanted to close her eyes and shut out the images his voice evoked, to still the shivers that slithered across the surface of her skin as memory provided a graphic reminder of the nights they'd spent in each other's arms.

'Tomorrow I fly north to Cairns for the photographic shoot at Port Douglas. I plan to stay on at the resort for a few days.' She managed to hold his gaze without wavering. 'I need some peace and tranquillity in my life.'

'You imagine I'll let you walk away?'

Pride, together with an innate sense of self-preservation, was responsible for the steadiness of her voice. 'There is nothing you can do to stop me.'

He stood looking at her for what seemed an age, and the breath caught in her throat, seeming to formulate into a lump which made it impossible for her to swallow.

Dark eyes hardened with frightening anger, and for one heart-stopping moment she thought he was going to *shake* her.

'Have your time alone, if that's what you think you need.' His voice was controlled, yet as hard as tensile steel. 'However, if you intend opting out of our impending marriage, then *you* must be the one to tell Jonathan and rescind all the arrangements.'

Lexi closed her eyes against the compelling sight of him, then slowly opened them again, aware of a primeval instinct for survival as she became trapped in the prison of his penetrating gaze.

'That amounts to emotional blackmail,' she said shakily.

'I'll use any tool I can.'

'*Why?*'

A faint, slightly cruel smile curved from the edge of his mouth. 'You think you have all the answers. Work it out for yourself.'

Without a further word he turned and walked to the door, opened it, then pulled it closed behind him.

Lexi lifted her hand in an involuntary gesture as her subconscious mind sought to call him back, then she shook her head and gazed sightlessly around the room.

Crossing her arms, she hugged them tightly against her breasts. Never before had she felt quite so frighteningly alone, bereft, and, with an aching sense of loss so acute it took every ounce of effort to walk to the door, she attached the safety chain, activated the alarm system, then made her way to bed.

CHAPTER ELEVEN

THE PORT DOUGLAS resort was aptly named Mirage, for that was how it appeared after an hour's drive from Cairns along a road that alternately hugged the coastal foreshore then swung inwards to weave its way through dense rainforest.

The heat hit Lexi the moment she stepped out from the air-conditioned limousine, the high humidity of a tropical wet season making the air seem heavy and stultifying, and tiny beads of sweat began to dew on her skin in the brief few minutes it took for her to pay the driver.

Her reserved suite was cool, decorated in pale muted shades that were visually restful, and as soon as she was alone she headed for the bathroom and stripped off her clothes.

A leisurely shower proved refreshing, and she selected shorts and a sleeveless top before extracting a bottle of pineapple juice from the refrigerator.

It was deliciously icy, and, sipping it slowly, she moved to the large sliding glass doors to view the lush sculptured grounds bounded by enormous palms, and, beyond, the wide expanse of ocean.

She should rest, she thought, have a quiet evening meal, and follow it with an early night, so that she would be ready to sparkle beneath the all-revealing eye of the camera first thing in the morning. Except that she felt impossibly restless, and she prowled round the suite, then crossed to the phone in a determined bid to ring Jonathan and tell him of her safe arrival.

Georg's name wasn't even mentioned, much to her relief, and after she'd replaced the receiver she stood staring at the telephone in brooding silence.

A discreet rap at the door provided an interruption, and she accepted the long slim cellophaned box from the delivery-man. As soon as she was alone she hurriedly tore open the accompanying envelope, only to discover that the flowers were from the management, welcoming her to the hotel.

A wry smile tugged at her mouth. Why shouldn't they make a token gesture? The publicity from this shoot would arouse tremendous interest in the resort.

And she desperately tried to ignore an inner voice taunting unmercifully that she should even dare hope Georg might have despatched a floral tribute.

Dear heaven, why was she so contrary? If the roses had come from Georg she probably would have given them to one of the staff. And why should he send her anything when she'd virtually walked out on him?

She clenched her hands, then winced as the stone from her engagement ring dug into her finger. And that was another thing, she thought wretchedly as she adjusted the ring so that it rested squarely. She should have taken the ring off and given it back to him before she left Sydney. Except that she hadn't, and she began to wonder why.

Damn. There were no easy answers, and she was darned if she was to embark on a fact-and-find soul-searching mission *now*.

She'd come here for a reason: to work, and to follow it with a few extra days of relaxation. And that was exactly what she intended to do. Georg, and every facet of her involvement with him, could be successfully put on hold.

But it wasn't that easy. At least *work* presented few difficulties. The cameraman was easy to work with, and the clothes were superb. It was afterwards, when she was alone, that the problems began, for with so much time on her hands she began to pursue a path of destructive introspection.

The days were bad enough, but the nights were worse, for then she lay awake, aware with each passing hour of a deep, aching sense of loss.

When she finally did manage to fall asleep her dreams were vivid and heart-rendingly graphic. Inevitably she came sharply awake to discover that Georg's presence was a figment of a fertile imagination, and reality was an empty bed.

To spend so much time alone was detrimental, Lexi decided, and in a desperate need to fill her days she embarked on every recommended tour available.

She made friends with a few fellow guests, joining them for dinner on two occasions, and she spoke to her father by phone every day.

However, the one call she wanted, more than any other, never came, and somehow she was unable to summon sufficient courage to make the call herself.

Why didn't Georg ring? she agonised at least a dozen times every day. Had he decided, after all, to believe all those hateful things she'd flung at him in temper? Perhaps he had used this last week for a bit of introspection of his own.

Oh, lord, it would be terribly ironic if *he* opted to call the wedding off, just when extensive self-analysis of her emotions revealed she'd fallen irretrievably in love with him. For there could be no doubt it was *love*.

There was only one way to find out, and with new-found resolve she rang the airline, booked the next flight south, then packed her bag and checked out of the hotel.

Lexi arrived in Sydney, collected her holdall, then hired a taxi to take her to Darling Point, where she retrieved her mail and took the lift up to her apartment.

The answering-machine held a variety of messages, and she played the tape as she sifted through her mail.

One of the first things she must do was ring Jonathan, she thought, for she didn't want to cause him any anxiety should he phone the Port Douglas resort only to be told she'd already left.

'Come visit me this evening,' her father bade her after they'd exchanged a preliminary greeting. 'Bring Georg.' She almost heard the laughter in his voice as he teased, 'I won't expect you to stay long.'

Oh, heavens, how did she get of that? 'Georg doesn't know I'm back yet,' she responded lightly. 'Can I take a raincheck, and make it tomorrow night? I'll ring you in the morning.'

As soon as she'd concluded the call she depressed the reset button and dialled Georg's number before she had time to give the action any thought. If she hesitated she'd never summon the necessary courage.

But he wasn't at the restaurant, nor was he in his office.

'Would you care to leave a message?'

She hesitated for all of five seconds. 'No, I'll ring back.'

Fool, she accorded the instant she replaced the receiver. It would have been much simpler if she'd left her name. Except that then *she* would be the one waiting with bated breath for the phone to ring, and if he didn't call she'd be totally shattered. At least this way the ball was still in her court.

Or was it? Somehow she couldn't help thinking he was playing a very shrewd game, deliberately allowing her to think she had her freedom, while all the time aware she could never truly be free of him.

At five o'clock she emerged from the shower, and after completing her toilette she took painstaking care with her appearance, choosing the expensive lace-edged silk teddy Georg had bid impossibly highly for to wear beneath a cream silk ensemble of culottes, matching top and jacket.

Make-up was deliberately subtle, with emphasis on her eyes and mouth, and she caught her hair up in an elaborate chignon from which she teased free a few wispy tendrils for effect.

The end result was startling, as she had intended, and without pause for thought she collected a clutch-bag, her car-keys, then stepped out from the apartment without so much as a backward glance.

Halfway to Georg's apartment she decided she was quite mad. For all she knew, he could be at the restaurant, or dining with Alex and Samantha. He could be in any one of a dozen places, and least of all was he likely to be home.

Yet she had to start somewhere, she decided as she parked the car and walked towards the elegantly designed foyer of his exclusive apartment block.

Depressing the appropriate intercom buzzer, she waited anxiously for a response.

'Carla. Who is there, please?'

'Lexi,' she relayed into the microphone. 'Lexi Harrison.'

'Mr Georg is not here. You want to come up?'

Relief washed over her. 'Please.'

The buzzer sounded, and the security door slid open. Three minutes later Lexi walked out from the lift into the penthouse lobby.

'Ah, there you are,' Carla greeted her in accented English within seconds of Lexi's pressing the doorbell. 'You are lucky I am still here. Tonight I am late in leaving.' A broad grin creased her attractive matronly features, and her eyes sparkled. 'You wait here for Mr Georg?'

'Yes.' Lexi preceded the housekeeper into the lounge and sank into one of the soft leather chairs. 'Is he going to be long?'

'I don't know.' An eloquent shrug lifted broad capable shoulders. 'He ring before and tell me he cook for himself tonight. You want I should get you something? A drink, maybe? I can fix you a snack.'

'No,' Lexi refused with a kindly smile. 'Thanks all the same; I'll be fine. You go.'

'You sure? It's no trouble.'

'Sure,' Lexi assured her, touched by the older woman's concern.

As soon as she was alone she rose to her feet and crossed to the huge glass window where she stood staring sightlessly out at the view.

The harbour glistened against a backdrop of city buildings and clear azure sky. A tugboat bustled importantly out to meet an incoming liner, and two ferries passed each other as they forged in opposite directions to their different destinations. Houses and apartment blocks dotted the foreshore, with trees and landscaped gardens covering numerous hills rising high from the sea.

In midsummer, with the advantage of daylight saving, there was still evidence of a heat haze lingering in the air, and it would be several hours before dusk would provide a gradually darkening shroud. Then the city would come alive with a galaxy of light, myriad pinpricks of electricity providing a veritable fairyland to complement the brilliantly flashing neon from city buildings.

It was a similar view to the one Lexi enjoyed from her own apartment, and she had become so accustomed to the visual beauty's being on constant display that it failed to register as she became lost in contemplation.

Would Georg be pleased to see her? Her features paled at the thought that he might not. Dear lord in heaven! How was she supposed to live without him? Oh, *why* did she have to suffer such a conflict of emotions? she cursed helplessly.

The faint sound of a key being turned in the lock momentarily froze her limbs, then she slowly swung round to face the door.

One glance at Georg's tall dark-suited frame was sufficient for the nerves in her stomach to begin a painful somersault, and she stood in mesmerised silence as he entered the room.

Her eyes flew to his face, seeing the dark set of his jaw, the broad chiselled cheekbones assembled into an unfathomable mask.

Everything she wanted to say remained locked in her throat, and she simply stood still as he carefully closed the door behind him.

Then he turned towards her, and she nearly died at the hard implacability evident.

'Lexi.'

His voice was a cynical world-weary drawl, and she drew a deep calming breath in defence against the agonising shaft of pain that ripped through her body.

'Hello, Georg,' she greeted him quietly, her eyes wide and clear as he moved further into the room. 'Carla let me in.'

He paused, surveying her with detached inscrutability for what seemed an age, then crossed to the drinks cabinet. 'Can I get you a drink?'

Lexi doubted she'd be able to lift the glass to her lips without spilling its contents, and if she so much as swallowed anything she'd choke! 'No—thanks,' she added with extreme politeness, watching as he selected a glass, added ice, a measure of whisky and a generous splash of soda before turning to face her.

'When did you get back?'

'This afternoon.'

He moved across to where she stood. 'You could have phoned.'

'I rang the office, but you weren't in.'

'A message would have reached me.'

The deep drawling voice sent goose-pimples scudding over the surface of her skin, and she had to steel herself against actually shivering. A spark of defiance lifted her chin and tilted it fractionally. 'You're not going to make this easy for me, are you?'

His eyes seared hers, hardening with frightening intensity. 'Can you give me any reason why I should?'

Lexi closed her eyes against the compelling sight of him, then slowly opened them again. The air between them seemed alive with latent emotion, and her heart gave a lurch as she glimpsed a muscle tensing along his jaw.

She was dangerously close to tears, and she looked at him, silently begging for his understanding. 'I spent every waking minute thinking about you while I was away, remembering, examining everything you said, all that had happened between us,' she began slowly. Her eyes unconsciously beseeched him to understand, but his expression remained an inscrutable mask. 'I even managed to persuade myself *before* Paul's revelation that marriage to you would have its compensations.' A hollow laugh rose in her throat to escape as a strangled sound, and she lifted her hands in a gesture of self-deprecation. 'Heaven knows, I'd rushed into my first marriage ignoring everything except my heart. There seemed to be some sense in using some caution with regard to a second attempt, and at least you had Jonathan's whole-hearted approval. I even dared to think we might be happy together, and I began to relax, lulled into a state of contented acceptance. I felt I could trust you, and I became very——' she hesitated, hardly wanting to lay bare her heart '—fond of you.' Oh, dear lord, if only he knew just *how* fond!

She waited for him to say something, to give her some reassurance, but he remained silent.

'After Paul, I didn't want to trust any man again. I didn't even feel I could trust myself.' She swallowed painfully, and felt the ache of unshed tears as she gathered the strength to continue. 'I hated having to live a lie, even for Jonathan's sake, and I especially hated you for taking me through the threshold of pain and showing me what pleasure could be.' Her mouth trembled as it tried for a smile and lost miserably. 'Must you have it all?' she demanded shakily, and it seemed a lifetime before he spoke.

'Yes.'

It took an inordinate amount of courage to continue, but she managed—just.

'When I discovered there was a deliberate conspiracy I was so angry, so disillusioned, so incredibly—hurt,' Lexi admitted poignantly.

His eyes never left hers for a second. 'And now?'

This was no time to be faint-hearted, and with a sense of trepidation she took the greatest gamble of her life. She lifted a shaky hand, then let it fall helplessly down to her side, and her eyes shimmered with the force of her emotion. 'I discovered I can't live without you.' She attempted a faint smile and failed miserably as her lips trembled. 'Don't you understand? *I love you.*' The words were torn out of her in a flow of wretched emotion, and she looked at him blindly through a well of tears. 'What more do you want?'

Georg carefully placed his glass down on a nearby table, then he caught hold of her shoulders and pulled her close, lifting a hand to catch hold of her chin and tilting it so that she had no option but to look at him.

'*You,*' he accorded softly. 'As my wife, by my side, always.'

There was no way she could still the silent trickling flow of tears as they spilled and ran slowly down each cheek, and her mouth shook almost beyond control.

His eyes darkened until they were almost black. 'Don't,' he groaned, gathering her close. '*Cristos*, don't cry!'

His hands were gentle as they slid through her hair to hold fast her head, and his mouth lowered to nuzzle the sweet curve of her neck, his lips caressing the softly throbbing vein until he felt the faint tremor in her throat; then he began a tantalisingly slow path to her mouth. He kissed her gently at first, then with increasing hunger as he sought to remove every last vestige of doubt.

It seemed an age before he relinquished her lips, and she could only look at him in total bemusement as he trailed a finger down the slope of her nose, and traced the soft, swollen contours of her mouth.

She was unable to prevent the slight shiver that raked her slender body, and he slid his hands up to frame her face.

'You're beautiful,' he accorded gently. 'So generous and warm and giving. A joy only a fool would discard.' He smiled as her eyes widened, and his thumb gently probed the tremulous curves of her mouth, then began tracing their outline with tactile exploration. 'It was impossible for me not to be aware of your existence,' he owned huskily. 'You intrigued me, and I wanted to get to know you better. Under normal circumstances Jonathan would have arranged for us to be formally introduced over dinner at his home, but both he and David knew you would see it as a deliberate guise. As soon as I learned of Jonathan's ill-health it was *my* suggestion to involve you in attempt to halt Paul's meddling.' His mouth moved to form a wry smile. 'I knew within days of going public with our supposed romance that only the reality would suffice, and I used every weapon at my command.' He laughed softly at her expression of disbelief. 'I knew I had insufficient time to afford you a gentle seduction. My pursuit had to be swift and blatant.' He paused to bestow a brief hard kiss to her soft mouth, thereby preventing any response she might have made. 'In my arms your body was its own traitorous mistress, alive and gloriously vibrant beneath my touch, and every time we made love I was sure you must know the extent of my feelings.' His lips touched hers, light and as fleeting as a butterfly's wings.

'I was sufficiently naïve to think it was merely sexual expertise,' Lexi admitted with a faint smile.

'I wanted to kill Paul,' Georg went on to reveal, and his eyes hardened with latent anger. 'A few days ago I had to physically restrain myself from going after him and committing serious bodily harm,' he asserted bleakly, and there was an inflexible quality evident in those tautly chiselled features that she longed to ease.

'It doesn't matter. *He* doesn't matter,' Lexi assured him, conscious of his darkening gaze.

'He'll never have the opportunity to hurt you again.'

She looked at him, loving the strength, the sheer animal magnificence that set him apart from other men. Her heart swelled, and her lips parted to form a soft tremulous smile.

'You're determined to play the role of my guardian angel?' she couldn't resist teasing, and received a husky growl in response as he gathered her close against him.

'Husband; lover,' he corrected, his expression softening miraculously, and she felt herself begin to drown in the warmth of his eyes. 'Friend; confidant,' he added, moulding her slim curves against his hardened frame. '*Yours*, for a lifetime.'

Her eyes clung to his, and for a moment she was unable to speak, then any words she might have said were lost as he lowered his head and kissed her with such gentle evocativeness that she almost cried.

'I love you,' he accorded gently. 'So much. These past few days have been hell. When I arrived home tonight and found you here I was so desperately afraid you had come to demand your freedom.'

Lexi lifted a hand to his lips, and her eyes widened measurably as he caressed each finger in turn, drawing first one, then the other into his mouth and gently biting each tender tip. A shaft of exquisite pleasure unfurled deep inside her, slowly radiating throughout her whole body until she was filled with delicious expectant warmth.

'Will you do something for me?'

His smile held such a degree of latent passion that she melted into a thousand pieces.

'What is this thing you want me to do?' He leaned forward and brushed his lips against the corner of her mouth in an evocative, deliberately tantalising gesture. 'Tell me.'

For a moment she almost hesitated, wondering if it was really important any more. 'Would you *ask* me to marry you?' Her voice was serious, and as he lifted his head she looked into his eyes, begging him to understand. In a defensive, unbidden gesture she edged the tip of her tongue over the soft curve of her mouth.

He stood regarding her in silence, his expression unusually grave. 'It means that much to you?'

'Yes.'

He caught hold of her hand and placed it against his chest so that she could feel the strong beat of his heart. 'Dear, sweet Lexi. Will you marry me? Let me love you, treasure you for the rest of my life?'

Her mouth shook a little, and her eyes ached with the wealth of her own emotion. 'Yes. *Yes*.' She slid her arms up round his neck and pulled his head down to hers. Then she kissed him, glorying in taking the initiative for a few long minutes before he became caught up with the strength of his own passion, wreaking a devastating assault on her feelings, plundering until she clung to him, unashamedly as anxious as he for a complete satiation of the senses.

It seemed an age before he slowly broke the kiss, and she gave a murmur in protest as he disentangled her arms from around his neck.

'Carla said you were going to cook,' she voiced reluctantly, wanting only to be close to him.

With infinite care he slid the jacket from her shoulders, then set about loosening her top.

'We'll have a midnight snack, and wash it down with champagne.' His hands slipped inside the waistband of her silk trousers and pushed them gently down over the slight curve of her hips. 'But right now all I want to do is feast myself on you,' he husked emotively, and she almost died at the wealth of passion evident in those dark eyes so close to her own.

Lexi gave a soft delighted laugh, and an inner radiance was responsible for the twinkle of utter bewitchment in the depths of her beautiful eyes. 'Here, in the lounge?'

With an exultant chuckle he swept her into his arms and carried her effortlessly down the hall to the master suite where he let her slip to her feet mere inches from the large bed.

'In my bed, minx,' he chided gently, shrugging out of his jacket in one easy movement. Her fingers began undoing the buttons on his shirt, dealing deftly with the belt buckle, and as she reached for the zip fastening on his trousers a long shudder shook his powerful frame.

Unbidden, she traced a slow pattern through the dark springy hair whorling on his chest, beginning a tactile exploration that brought a strangled sound from the depths of his throat.

'Do you have any conception of what you're doing to me?'

A shaft of exquisite pleasure exploded deep within her, radiating through every nerve until she felt incredibly alive, for it was a heady experience to imagine she held any power over him.

'I think the feeling is mutual,' she managed shakily some minutes later as his lips trailed an evocative path to her breasts, and she cried out as his tongue savoured one taut roseate peak, then drew it gently between his teeth to suckle, creating such delicious torture that it was almost impossible not to cry out at the degree of ecstacy spiralling through her body.

Gently he pulled her down on to the bed, and their loving became a long slow pacing of each other's pleasure that surpassed anything they'd previously shared.

Afterwards they rose and shared a leisurely bath, delighting in creating new depths of sensual arousal, and it was a long time later, cradled close in the protective circle of Georg's arms, that Lexi lifted her head towards his to voice quietly, 'Thank you.'

His lips trailed gently across her forehead to settle at her temple. 'For what, specifically?'

'Loving me,' she accorded simply. She felt his mouth begin a slow caressing path down to her cheek until it reached the curve of her lips.

'You're so unbelievably beautiful that you take my breath away.'

She smiled beneath the witching touch of his mouth, and a delicious laugh bubbled to the surface. 'Do you think you can summon sufficient energy to sizzle two steaks while I toss a salad?'

'*Sizzle?*' He caught her lower lip between his teeth in subtle punishment, and growled softly, 'A gourmet chef creates magic with food.'

'Not merely with food,' she declared solemnly, slipping easily from his grasp, but only, she suspected, because he let her.

She walked unselfconsciously into the *en suite* bathroom and plucked a large bath-sheet to wrap sarong-style round her slim curves, then she emerged into the bedroom to see he'd risen from the bed and was in the process of donning a silk robe.

Georg held out his hand and she placed hers into that strong warm enveloping grasp, then together they walked out of the room.

All the self-doubts, the pain, were gone, and in its place was love—everlasting.

A Year DOWN UNDER

WORDFIND #2

```
A  U  S  T  R  A  L  I  A  T  Y  I  O  B
F  A  V  K  L  I  E  Y  K  R  D  F  V  I
Z  X  C  V  N  M  X  V  Q  E  H  G  S  A
P  I  U  Y  R  B  I  T  Y  T  J  K  L  N
S  E  D  U  C  T  I  O  N  F  Q  L  B  C
G  N  H  R  B  K  H  E  I  Z  T  E  P  H
R  X  F  A  U  I  M  B  U  Q  W  D  I  I
O  A  Y  P  R  E  T  E  N  D  S  O  T  N
E  Q  U  W  G  R  A  Q  W  I  J  M  R  A
G  L  I  A  E  R  I  T  H  L  K  X  Q  W
Q  Z  G  C  V  N  M  S  H  T  L  A  E  W
L  N  Y  L  O  N  I  C  O  L  A  O  S  N
E  A  S  D  L  K  J  H  T  N  Y  U  I  O
D  Y  H  L  Y  E  N  D  Y  S  G  D  M  X
```

AUSTRALIA	MODEL
BIANCHIN	NICOLAOS
ENGAGEMENT	PRETEND
GEORG	SEDUCTION
HARRISON	SYDNEY
LEXI	WEALTH

Look for A YEAR DOWN UNDER Wordfind #3
in March's Harlequin Presents #1537,
THE GOLDEN MASK by Robyn Donald

WF2

HARLEQUIN ◆ PRESENTS®

A Year DOWN UNDER

In 1993, Harlequin Presents celebrates the land down under. In March, let us take you to Northland, New Zealand, in THE GOLDEN MASK by Robyn Donald, Harlequin Presents #1537.

Eden has convinced herself that Blade Hammond won't give her a second look. The grueling demands of trying to keep the sheep station running have left her neither the money nor the time to spend on pampering herself. Besides, Blade still considers her a child who needs protecting. Can Eden show him that she's really a woman who needs his love . . . ?

Share the adventure—and the romance— of A Year Down Under!

SOLUTIONS TO
WORDFIND #2